Double Trouble

I0621450

Jacob's Brides

J L Dawson

Double Trouble

Jacob's Brides

Book 10

By J L Dawson

Butterfly Books

PUBLISHING

Cover design by: Virginia McKevitt

ISBN (Paperback) 978-1-7386017-2-1
ISBN (E-book) 978-1-7386017-3-8

A CiP catalogue record for this title is available from the National Library of New Zealand.

First edition, 2023 Butterfly Books Publishing

Contact the author or subscribe to newsletter:
jldawsonauthor@yahoo.com
www.jodawsonauthor.com

Contents

One

"I told you we were going to be late." Jacob Jenkins scowled at his brother, gesturing to the churchyard and the many wagons waiting. "Why do you always have to preen yourself like a peacock?"

"I don't preen." Jarrod frowned.

Jake raised his brows as he pulled Scout to a stop and jumped down from the gig. "You spent twenty minutes just on your hair." He tethered the horse and fetched his Bible from under the seat.

Jarrod climbed over the side. Then he took a moment to smooth his clothing and slid his hands over his slicked-back hair. "Gotta look good for the ladies."

Jake rolled his eyes before punching his younger brother on the arm. "You're a fool. Aint no lady gonna want a man that reeks of pomade and smells like he's been swimming in a vat of cologne."

"Easy for you to say. You've already got a girl." Jarrod scowled as they walked toward the church.

This brought a stupid grin to Jake's face. "Sure do."

Jarrod shook his head and scoffed. "You've got it bad. When're you gonna propose anyway?"

Jake raised his brows and scratched his chin as they reached the door. "Trust me, Brother."

Jarrod shook his head again and a wry smile crossed his face. They slunk into the back seats as the congregation stood to sing the opening hymn.

"Amazing Grace..." Jake's deep voice raised in praise to the Lord. As he sang, his eyes roved the church until he spotted the woman he loved sitting near the front with her parents. He grinned. Even from the back she was a beautiful woman. She had pinned her dark hair up with his hair comb holding it in place.

Jake's face lit up. *Today is set to be the beginning of my happy ever after.* He was glad to see she was wearing her favorite blue dress, the one that made her eyes shine.

The song finished and he tried to focus on the service but the closer he got to the town picnic the more nervous he became, and he couldn't drag his eyes off the back of her head.

At last the service finished and Jake shook his head as his brother made a bee-line to a group of young ladies who stood chatting in the corner. He stood as the woman he loved walked toward him on her father's arm.

She smiled at him and he felt his heart skip. He nodded to Mr. Adams and the man released his daughter's arm. A nostalgic smile crossed the older man's face, and he sighed as she took Jake's arm.

"Good morning, Christina."

"Hi, Jake." She squinted and looked from his beaming face to her father's wistful look. "What's going on?"

Jake lifted his elbow to her. "Nothing at all, will you let me escort you to the town picnic?"

Christina took one more look at her father's face and nodded slowly. "Alright." Her suspicions raised. She turned her back on her family and allowed Jake to lead her from the church.

They sat together with Christina's parents, and her older brother Mark and his wife Tina, enjoying their lunch.

They finished eating, and Jake lent a hand, packing up their lunch. He looked across the common to see his brother chatting with Millie Ellis. He shook his head with a sly grin on his face. It was a different girl each week for Jarrod. Still, he prayed for his brother. There was nothing better than having a steady girl and falling in love.

Jake could bear it no more. The ring was burning a hole in his pocket. Standing, he put his hand out to Christina. She took it and stood up. He grinned at her. "Will you go for a brief walk with me? I'll take you home afterward."

The gleam in his eyes made her blush. "Certainly. Let me just tell Pa."

He nodded, and she ran to her father, who was packing the wagon. He sighed and nodded, looked up at Jake, and gave him a nod and a nostalgic smile.

Christina hurried back to Jake and took his offered hand. "Where do you want to go?"

"Just over to the lake." He gestured to the small lake at the edge of the common.

She nodded and smiled and they fell into step with each other, walking in silence until they reached a little sheltered bay; a favorite fishing spot for many in the town.

They stopped and looked over the water for a time, but neither spoke.

Jake took a deep breath and exhaled loudly. Christina dropped his arm and turned to look at him. "What is it?"

He took her hand and stroked her cheek. "I love you, Chrissy."

Christina nodded and raised her brows. "I know that, I love you too. Is that why you wanted to bring me here?"

Jake's heart raced and pounded in his ears. He could feel his whole body shaking. "No... I ahh..." He sighed.

"What is it, Jake? You're frightening me."

Jake closed his eyes. "I'm sorry, I don't mean to." *Lord, give me strength.* After his quick prayer he opened his eyes, put his hand in his pocket, and fell to one knee. He grinned and lifted the box to her.

Christina's eyes grew wide and her mouth dropped open. A slight squeal escaped her lips and her eyes flooded with tears.

Jake kissed the delicate hand he held and looked up at her sparkling blue eyes. "Chrissy, you're so beautiful and lovely, and you've captured my heart. I'm nothing but a rancher with a heart full of love, but I offer it all to you."

Christina tucked her lips under and lifted her hand to her chest.

"Christina June Adams, will you marry me?" Jake was certain she could feel him shaking. His whole body was on fire. The silence between them was deafening. It was the longest half a second of his life.

Christina smiled widely. "Of course, Jake. Oh, of course I'll marry you."

Jake leapt up and jumped in the air, clicking his heels together. He ran a circle right around her then took her in his arms and lifted her in the air. Christina flung her arms around his neck and they shared a sweet kiss. He pulled back from her, still holding her off her feet so they were face to face. "I love you, Chrissy. I can't wait to marry you."

"I love you too, Jake." Her eyes shone. "May I see that ring?"

Jake chuckled and put her back on her feet. He pulled out the ring and slipped it on her finger. Christina lifted her hand to inspect it. "Oh, Jake, it's so lovely."

"I chose it for the pretty blue stone. I know you love blue."

"It's pretty, thank you."

Jake lifted the hand that bore his ring and kissed it. "You're welcome. Come on, shall we tell the others?" He put his arm out to her.

"Absolutely."

"Jarrod's gonna be so jealous. He still can't believe I'd get a girl before he did. He fancies himself rather a dandy."

Christina laughed. "I know, he was in my grade and even back then he was always chasing the girls."

"I hope he'll settle down one day and just be himself." Jake winked at Chrissy. "Worked for me."

"Did it just?" She tipped her head and squinted at him.

"You said yes to me remember?"

"Yes I did." She squeezed his arm and chuckled as they entered the common.

Two

"I can't wait for Jake to see me in my new gown." Christina grinned at her mother, seated next to her in the stagecoach. There were two men sitting opposite them, both reading newspapers. "It's the first silk I've ever owned, and the lilac is so beautiful."

"He will in two weeks, Darling. You'll knock his stockings off when he sees you."

"I hope so." Her cheeks reddened at the thought. "I feel bad about the cost, though."

"You mustn't feel bad, Darling. Your pa gave us the money, and he wants you to have the gown you want. You've opted to do everything else with little cost, and you deserve to have the dress you want."

"I did pick one I could wear to dances and maybe to church."

Mrs. Adams furrowed her brows. "I'm not sure it's appropriate for church. It's a tad elaborate."

"You're right." Christina grinned. She turned to look out the window. Wide Dakota grasslands stretched before her. Occasionally they'd travel through a grove of trees or a small settlement, but most of the journey would be across open prairie land.

They approached a vast area of shrubland next to a small lake on the outskirts of Hopes Brook. Christina stretched her neck. "There's the lake, Ma, only a few miles to home."

Mrs. Adams opened her mouth to speak but gunshots stole her words. Both women's eyes grew wide, and the men dropped their papers and looked out the windows.

They heard a yell, and the driver fell from the coach. The horses began their stampede, causing the stagecoach to fling its passengers from side to side. The door flew open and one of the men was thrown out when the stage lurched to the side. Mrs. Adams was knocked to the floor and hit her head on the hard wood floor. Christina screamed and gripped the seat until her knuckles turned white. Another gunshot caused a loud whinny and the stage stopped abruptly, causing it to tip over on its side.

Thrown across the coach, Christina fell firmly against the door. She saw blood oozing from her mother's head. "Ma..."

"Don't make a sound. Play dead," the remaining man whispered to a wide-eyed Christina.

She nodded and closed her eyes tightly as two men poked their heads into the stage. She listened as they bickered amongst themselves and hauled the three of them out. She kept her body limp as a man roughly grabbed her and dragged her up out of the overturned stage.

"Earnest! Get this one, they's all dead."

The man threw her roughly down to the man below. She felt the wind go out of her as he manhandled her to the ground. She landed on her back with one arm tucked underneath her. It was agonising but she didn't dare move. She felt the body of her mother fall on top of her.

"This one's still alive," a voice yelled and a gunshot rang out.

Another body landed across Christina's legs. He was heavy and she was sure her foot would break under his weight. She shuddered internally at the realization that the two bandits had killed him without hesitation. She absolutely could not let them know she was still alive.

"Search 'em, take whatever'll fetch a price," the same voice called. "I'll start on the bags."

Christina kept her eyes tightly closed as she felt the body of the man, and her mother dragged off her. She felt a hand reach down and snatch the cameo off her neck. *Lord help me.* She prayed and determinedly remained still and limp.

The crook yanked her engagement ring from her finger and she stifled the urge to cry out.

He turned toward his brother, missing the grimace Christina was unable to hide. "Marv, got me some jewels, and the fella had a tidy sum on 'im." He lifted a stack of money in the air and smirked.

"Come an' 'elp me wit the bags, we gotta get outta 'ere," his brother called.

Christina heard him move away from her. She dared to open one eye just a little. They were too busy hauling out bags and trunks to notice her. She opened her eyes wider and watched them. They were obviously twins and looked almost identical except that one had a moustache and the other a moustache and goatee. She etched their faces firmly in her mind, determined to remember them.

She sighed quietly, as they tore her new gown from its trunk and threw it on the ground in their harried search for anything of value. She closed her eyes tightly again, praying for God to save her. At last, she heard the men run into the trees with their treasures and hoofbeats gallop away.

Her head swirled, and the weight still pressing on her body was agonising. She was almost positive she had a broken rib. "Help me, Lord," she whispered before the world went black.

*   *   *   *

Sheriff Kelly rode out of Hopes Brook to meet the stage and escort it to town. There'd been a spree of stage robberies in the area and he wanted to check up on it. He hadn't bothered to leave early; the stage was notoriously late.

He approached the small lake and gasped, nudging Lucky into a gallop. "Oh, no." He noticed the upturned stagecoach and the two dead horses.

Leaping off, he knelt before the man who'd been thrown from the coach. He sighed and shook his head. There was no point in checking the driver for a pulse. The blood on his shirt and bullet hole in his chest gave away his fate.

The sheriff ran to the pile of bodies, he knelt and checked the pulse of the man, shaking his head he cussed under his breath. Assuming they were all dead he stood up and pressed his palm to his forehead. Closing his eyes he shook his head sadly. A low, pitiful groan turned him around and he noticed Christina move just ever so slightly.

"Ohhh my! I'm here!" He shoved the man off Christina and picked up her mother, who was sadly deceased. Kneeling next to Christina, he touched her shoulder. "Miss Adams, can you hear me? Miss Adams?"

"Whhhhaaaa." Christina's eyes remained closed and she groaned again.

"Miss Adams, it's Sheriff Kelly. You're okay."

"No, get off me, don't touch me!" She sat up abruptly almost striking the sheriff on the chin. "Get away from me," she yelled again and put her arms over her face, groaning loudly as a splitting pain pulsed through her ribs.

"It's okay, It's me, Sheriff Kelly. You're safe."

"Ohhhhh." She sucked in heaving breaths. "Mama?"

Sheriff Kelly touched her shoulder gently. "I'm sorry, she's gone."

"Ohhhhh." Tears flooded her eyes, and she sobbed into her hands. The sheriff squeezed her shoulder and let her cry. "Oh, Sheriff Kelly, it was so horrible."

"Come on, Miss Adams, I'll get you back to town, to the doc, then I'll set to helping these poor souls."

Christina looked at him with sad eyes and merely nodded. She tried to stand, but groaned loudly.

"Don't try to stand, I'll help you up."

Three

Jake sighed loudly and removed his hat as he drove onto the ranch at long last. Thrusting his fingers through his hair, he looked up as his brother rode toward him.

"What kept you?" Jarrod groaned. "You've been gone five days. I thought you said it'd only be three?"

Jake grimaced and pulled the team alongside Jarrod's horse. He gestured to the load on the back of the wagon, bound securely under the canvas. "It took me longer to find what I wanted than I thought. I got all the supplies for the ranch, but..." His cheeks reddened and a wide smile crossed his face. "I wanted to get my bride a gift for our new house." Jake nodded toward the small home situated near the grander ranch house.

Jarrod shook his head and raised his eyebrows. "I thought you had everything you needed. You said the house was ready."

"It is, this is a special gift just for Chrissy."

"What is it?"

"A sewing machine."

Jarrod raised his brows and nodded. "That's quite a gift, Brother."

"Yeah, I sold the old hog, remember? I used a little of the money to purchase this." He gestured to the back of the wagon as they pulled up in front of the barn. "She's absolutely worth every penny. I know she's gonna love it. She can't take her ma's machine. Mrs. Adams is a seamstress. She needs it to make a living. I thought Chrissy deserves one of her own. I can't wait to surprise..."

Both men's heads jerked around at the sound of galloping hooves. They looked at each other and frowned. Both hurriedly dismounted as the sheriff skidded to a halt.

"Sherrif." Jake put his hand hesitantly out to the man as he jumped off his horse. He seldom rode at such a break-neck speed.

"Jake, I'm glad I caught you. Your brother told me he expected you home a few days ago."

"I just got in now, Sheriff. I was delayed somewhat. What can I do for you?"

The sheriff swallowed hard. Being the bearer of sad news was the hardest part of his job. "I ahhh. Umm." He sighed loudly, removed his hat, and ran his fingers through his greasy hair. "Well... that is... I need to talk to you. It's rather urgent, I'm afraid."

"Certainly. I'll be heading to town shortly to see Chrissy, but I need to clean up first. I'm sure Ma's got the coffeepot on. Come on in, Sheriff."

"I'll see to the team." Jarrod reached for the rein, noticing the intensity in the sheriff's eyes.

Sheriff Kelly grimaced and shook his head ever so slightly and followed Jake into the house.

"Thank you, Mrs. Jenkins." The sheriff nodded to the slight woman and took the coffee cup from her outstretched hand.

"Most welcome, Sheriff. There's cookies and I'll leave the coffeepot." She passed a second cup to her son. "I'll leave you gentlemen to your conversation."

Jake winked at his mother and she scurried out of the room. He grinned at the sheriff. "I'm sure gonna miss having Ma take care of me, but I guess I'll have my lovely wife and that's even better..." He stopped abruptly as the sheriff closed his eyes and shook his head. "Sheriff?" Jake lowered his coffee cup and reached for a cookie.

"I'm not sure where to begin, Jake."

The look on the sheriff's face made Jake's heart leap into his chest. "Has something happened? You look like you've seen a ghost."

The sheriff took a long draft of his coffee and exhaled loudly. "I better just say it." He lifted an envelope from his pocket and slid it across the table.

Jake glanced at it. He recognised Chrissy's rapid script on the front. He frowned. "What is this?"

"I'll explain, Son." Another large mouthful of coffee soothed the sheriff's nerves somewhat and he began. "I'm sorry to say, there's been an accident."

Jake's coffee cup hovered in mid-air. "What's it got to do with Chrissy? Is she alright?"

*   *   *   *

Jake sat on the porch of his new home and looked out over the open range. He gasped in deep breaths and swiped at the tears trailing down his cheeks. His

14

eyes grew far away, and Chrissy's letter lay discarded on the small table next to him.

"Jake?"

Jake's head jerked up as his best friend rode up. Eli jumped off his horse and flicked the rein over the hitching rail.

Jake swiped at his eyes again and tried desperately to keep the tremble from his lips.

His friend slumped into the second chair. "Sheriff said you'd gotten some news and might need to talk. He wouldn't tell me what it was. Ya look like you've had your heart torn out. What's going on?"

Jake let out a single sob and thrust the harried letter at his friend. Eli read the note and his face fell. He snapped his head up to look at his friend. "What does this mean? She's gone, just like that?"

Jake merely nodded.

"Why?"

"Keep reading." They were the first words Jake had uttered since the sheriff left. He'd not even spoken to any of his family. They knew him well; he'd brood for a day or so then he'd come around. Still, Jarrod would stay the night at the cabin with him. He instinctively knew his brother shouldn't be alone. He promised. He'd be by after supper.

Eli read aloud. "... *I know this isn't easy to hear, but I'm afraid the sheriff has given me no choice. Pa and I are being sent away. He said it's for our own protection. The men who robbed the stage and killed Mama are dangerous and notorious men and if they find out that I'm the one who gave them up they'll be likely to come after me. The*

Marshalls will come for us tonight. I wish you were home so I could at least say goodbye. I don't know how long we'll be gone, it may be years. They have to find these men and apprehend them and then there'll be trials and it could all take some time. I don't know where we'll be, and the Marshalls won't tell us until we arrive at our destination.

Please know I'll always love you.
Your, Chrissy.

Eli closed his eyes and shook his head.

Hearing the words again, Jake broke down in sobs. Eli reached across and put his hand on his friend's shoulder. "I'm sorry. You'll have to postpone the wedding then?"

Jake sat up and sniffed loudly. "Sheriff said there can't be a wedding. I have to let her go and move on." His voice was low and raspy. He took a deep breath and wiped his eyes with his sleeve.

"What're ya gonna do?"

Jake fixed his dark eyes on Eli and shrugged. "Nothing I can do, they've been hidden away for her safety. Guess I just gotta get on with my life." He exhaled loudly and swiped away a tear.

"Are you sure she won't be back? Can you at least write to her?"

Jake shrugged. "Sheriff said I can't know where she is. If we were married it'd be different, I coulda gone with her. Even Mark and Tina aren't allowed to know. The worst part is she's lost her ma and I can't even comfort her." He sucked in three rapid breaths and broke down in sobs again.

Eli gripped his friend's shoulder until he sat up again.

"It's my fault."

"How's that?" Eli frowned and placed the letter on the small table.

"She was in the city getting her wedding gown. If it weren't for me, she wouldn't have been on that stage. I was supposed to go with them. If it hadn't been for my trip I'd've been with them. Then I coulda kept her safe..."

"Or you'd be dead too."

Jake nodded. "Might be better than this agony."

"What if she'd lived but lost both of you? Then what?"

Jake nodded again and both men sat in silence for a time. "I'm sorry, Jake. I know you love her."

"I don't understand why God would do this. Two weeks and we'd've been living here together. Not sure I can live here without her." He gestured to the house behind him.

Eli could do nothing but nod. A large crate caught his eye. "What's in the crate?" He attempted to change the subject.

Jake shrugged. "Sewing machine I brought for Chrissy."

Eli shook his head. "I'm sorry. Want me to help you take it inside?"

"Can't. I can't have it in there. It'll just remind me of what I've lost."

"Are you sure you've lost her? She could come back."

"Sheriff told me not to count on it, said it could take years, she'll have moved on by then for sure."

"And you will too, in time."

Jake shrugged. "I'm not so sure."

Eli merely nodded again; there were no words to comfort his friend. The pain was too fresh for Jake. Eli prayed in time God would mend his friend's broken heart.

Four

"I think you should still ask him. He won't thank you for keeping it from him, no matter how much he's hurting." Elsie Jenkins looked up from her knitting.

"He's in a dark place, Ma, I don't want to feel like I'm rubbing salt in his wounds."

"Jarrod, it's been more'n a year. He'll come through it all. You don't have to feel bad about your happiness."

Jarrod couldn't help but grin. "I can't wait to marry Viola-Jane. I can't help but think how I'd feel in Jake's shoes...." He paused and grimaced as his brother walked in, and thrust his hat on the hook.

"Don't stop on my account." Jake scowled. "Ya aren't in my shoes are ya?"

Jarrod stood. "I wanted to ask a favor."

"Yeah." Jake raised his brows and folded his arms over his chest.

"Vi's agreed to marry me."

"Good for you." Jake scowled.

"Jake, I know you're hurtin', Son, but you can be happy for your brother." Elsie stood up and put her hand on her oldest son's shoulder.

Jake started to protest and then shrugged and sighed. "Yeah, I'm pleased for you, Jarr. Least one of us should be happy."

"Jake, you will be happy again, in time, I know it. You just gotta let your heart heal."

Jake sneered at his brother. "When will that be?"

"Can't answer that, but you need to turn to God. He'll bring along the right woman in time." His mother squeezed his arm.

"I thought He already had."

"Son, you have to find a way to let Chrissy go."

Jake closed his eyes and sighed. "I'm trying, Ma, but I love her. I'll always love her I guess."

"Of course you will, Son. But every day you get a little better, and one day you'll let someone new in."

"So what was it you wanted to ask me?" Jake eyed his brother.

"Well, we aren't gonna wait; we're gonna get married in a week. I want to know if you'll stand up with me. I understand if you don't want to, but I'd really like you there with me."

Jake shrugged. "I guess. If ya want me."

Jarrod smiled. "Of course I do. You're my brother."

"Where're ya gonna live?"

"We're still deciding. I don't wanna be too far from the ranch."

"You can have my cabin." Jake raised and lowered one shoulder and ran his fingers through his hair.

Jarrod frowned. "Come on, we can't take your house."

"You might as well. I aint living there. I built that home for Chrissy. Can't live there without her. I never spent but the one night there since she left. It just reminds me of all I lost. She's the one that decorated it. Please, have the house. I'll stay on here with Ma."

"Are you sure?"

Jake smiled for the first time. "Yeah, one of us should be happy at least. Tell Vi to make it her own. She might as well have the sewing machine I brought for Chrissy too."

Jarrod shook his head. "I really am sorry, Jake."

"Ain't your fault." Jake shrugged. "I'll be okay. I really want you to have the house and the sewing machine. Please, I'll feel better knowing the house is being used, at least."

Jarrod nodded and embraced his brother. "Thank you. And for what it's worth. I'm praying for you."

Jake stood back and nodded, pursing his lips together.

* * * *

"What's on your mind, Son?"

Jake swallowed his mouthful of roast beef and potatoes and gave his mother a sad smile. "Just feeling sorry for myself. Jarrod's married, and happy and...." He sighed loudly.

Elsie reached across and squeezed his arm. "I understand, Son. I still get lonesome thinking of ya pa and he's been gone nearly ten years."

Jake nodded. "I miss him."

"You're so much like him, Jake, he'd be proud of how ya running the place."

"Thanks, Ma, I hope so. I always wanted him to be proud of me."

"I know he never said much, but he was proud of both of ya. He wasn't good at saying what he felt, even to me. But when he got sick and it looked like he wouldn't make it, he told me that the ranch would be in good hands. You were both young but with Charlie to help ya, you've done a fine job with the ranch. And you've looked after me. I'm glad."

"I guess it's a silver lining to me not being married, Ma, I can be here with you. I don't want ya being alone."

"I'm confident it'll happen for you. You're a young man and you'll have a family someday. Ya needn't worry about me, I'll be just fine."

"No way, Ma. Pa made me swear I'd always look after you. I gave him my word."

Elsie smiled and patted her son's hand. "Thank you, Dear. You're the best son a mother could've asked for. I do wish to see you happy, though."

"I will be, one day, I'm sure." Jake shrugged and let out a loud sigh.

"It's been nearly sixteen months. Maybe you need to look for a new sweetheart."

He shrugged again. "I don't know. It wouldn't be fair to a woman while I'm still in love with Chrissy."

Elsie patted his hand again. "When the Lord brings along the right girl, He'll replace ya feelings."

Jake leaned over and kissed his mother on the forehead. "In the meantime, you're my best girl. Thanks for looking after me so well, Ma. I love you."

"I love you too, Son. I pray every day for the Lord to bring you a generous, loving woman."

"Thanks for your faith in me."

"Of course, Jake. I'm proud of you too." She stood and reached for his plate. "Now come and help me with the washin' up."

Jake smiled. "Yes, Ma'am. Then I'll hitch the gig and take you to town."

"Very good."

* * * *

Jake helped his mother down from the gig and reached up for the basket. "Want me to carry the basket for you, Ma?"

"Nah, Son, you see to your errands. I'll be just fine."

"Okay. I'll take you to lunch afterward if you like?" He nodded to the café across the street. "I'd like to try out Hannah-Mae's new cherry cake. Jarr was raving about it last week."

"I'd like that."

Jake nodded and lifted his hand to help his mother up the stairs into the store. He winked at her and walked toward the farm supplies store.

"Morning, Jake."

Lifting his head Jake gave his friend a smile. "Eli, how's business?"

Eli gestured to the livery before him. "Fairly busy, I got four new horses, and I'm needing some more space, thinking of getting a new stable built."

"That's good, I'm glad things are going well for you."

Eli turned his eyes past Jake and grinned without meaning to. His face lit up and Jake raised his brows and turned to follow his gaze. He looked at his friend's beaming face. Giving Eli a knowing nod, he scratched his chin. "Sylvia Moore?"

Eli's cheeks colored and he flashed his friend a wry smile as the petite woman disappeared into the mercantile.

"You love her, don't you?"

"Yep, the pastor agreed to let me call on her. We've been courtin' a little over a week."

Jake nodded and gripped his shoulder. "Congratulations," he said non-committally, ending with a loud sigh.

Eli nodded. "Sorry, Jake, I don't mean to flaunt my happiness."

Jake shrugged one shoulder. "Don't be sorry. It's been sixteen months, I need to get used to it, I'm happy for you."

"Thanks, it'll happen for you too."

"I'm not holding my breath."

"Don't lose hope, there'll be someone for you. If I can find a girl, so can you."

"I'm not ready for anyone yet. I may never be." Jake shrugged again and shoved his hands in his pockets. "Someone's gotta look after Ma, so it's just as well I guess."

"I wish you'd come to the dance."

"Are you going?"

"Sylvia wants me to, it'll be our first real outing, even persuaded me to get a new suit."

Jake raised his brows and grinned. "You really do love her, never thought I'd hear of you dressing up like that."

Eli chuckled. "I'm even planning to get a shave and a haircut."

"I guess I should be thankful I don't have to worry. Ain't no one to care if I got whiskers or not."

"Still, you should come. Most'a the town'll be there."

Jake shrugged. "Ain't got no one to go with, save Ma."

"You know there are plenty of single chaps in this town that attend. This is the first time I've had a lady to take."

Jake sighed and ran his fingers through his hair. "Yeah, I'll come. Not sure I'll dance with anyone, but I'll come and make an appearance, Ma'll wanna be there, at least for a short time."

"Well, I better get back to work. Got eight horses to shoe today." Eli grimaced.

"I'll leave you to it. See you tomorrow night."

Eli nodded and turned back to his livery. Jake continued to the farm supplies store. He saw to his business, arranged for his purchases to be delivered and walked out.

He stopped abruptly as he noticed a small patch of wildflowers growing next to the boardwalk. He smiled and walked over to pick a small handful to give to his mother. "Well at least I have a lady to bring flowers to, even if it is just Ma." He smirked. The clock on the bank struck midday. Jake turned abruptly to hurry toward the café crashing straight into a young woman walking out of the bank, sending her sprawling off the boardwalk onto the road.

"Ohhhh." He thrust the flowers on the rough boardwalk and jumped down. "I'm so sorry, Miss." He knelt next to her as she sat up. "I'm so sorry. I wasn't watching where I was going."

"That's okay, I was daydreaming. I didn't see you there."

"No the fault is completely mine. I beg your forgiveness, Ma'am."

She looked up and smiled kindly at him. "There's no need. It was an accident."

He sucked in a breath, noticing she had two different-colored eyes. He put a hand out and gently touched her arm. The lurch in his heart took him by surprise. He'd never met a person who looked like her before. She was very petite with red hair twisted like a coiled rope on the back of her head and the most amazing eyes that he couldn't stop staring at. One shimmering green with brown flecks, the other a clear sky blue.

He tried to speak but wasn't able to. He paused with his hand on her shoulder.

She smiled shyly and lowered her head, breaking the spell, her cheeks growing a deep red.

"Ahhh. Let me help you up, Ma'am," he stammered at last. "Are you hurt?"

"I think I twisted my ankle, but it's not too bad. If you could just help me up, I'll be okay."

"I'm sorry." Jake frowned, overwhelmed with compassion for this stranger. "Let me help you to the doc, just to be sure."

"I'm sure that's not necessary, Mister?"

He smiled. "The names Jenkins, Jacob Jenkins." He put an arm around her and helped her stand. She winced and lifted her sore foot to rest on her toes.

"Ohh." She groaned and leaned against his arm.

"Let me get you to the infirmary. That's a worse twist than you thought. Please allow me?" He looked at her and gulped again. Her intriguing eyes pierced his soul.

She nodded and gave him a shy smile. He scooped her up into his arms, and she flung hers around his neck. The feeling caused his heart to lurch again and he let out a slight groan without meaning to.

"I'm sorry, am I heavy?" She blushed.

He shook his head, "Not at all, you're as light as a feather." His voice trembled. Her perfume and her proximity made his heart pound in his ears. He froze as she fixed her eyes on his again and smiled. Her lips were the brightest pink and full, and he had to fight the urge to kiss her.

"Mr. Jenkins, are you alright?"

"Um... Yeah... Um... that is..." He exhaled and reluctantly dragged his eyes from hers, before his resolve crumbled. "Come on, I'll get you to the doc," he managed, thankful for the distraction.

Eli wiped his brow and looked up, he shook his head as he watched Jake picking flowers. "For his mother, no doubt." He chuckled and then paused as Jake knocked down the lovely young woman who'd just walked out of the bank. "I wonder who she is?" he said aloud and then grinned again as he noticed his friend pause. He nodded. "I think you're beginning to heal, my friend." He chuckled again and walked back into his livery.

"Doc," Jake called and placed the woman down on the bed.

Doctor Peterson walked out of the next room wiping his hands on a towel. "Mr. Jenkins. Who's this?"

Jake stepped back and shrugged, his cheeks colored and he went to speak, embarrassed to realize he'd not got her name.

She smiled at the doctor. "I'm Lydia Howard, I'm new in town."

The doctor reached the bed and nodded.

Jake found his voice. "I'm afraid I knocked her down. I think she's twisted her ankle."

"Thank you, Mr. Jenkins. I'll take it from here."

"Very well." Jake turned his eyes back to Lydia. "I hope you're okay, Miss Howard." He nodded to the doctor. "I'll be by to fix up the bill later."

Before the doctor could respond, Lydia protested, "There is no need Mr. Jenkins."

Jake paused and touched her arm. He smiled kindly and looked into her unusual eyes. "It's the least I can do, Miss Howard, since I knocked you down. It's what a gentleman does, it's only right."

Lydia's wide smile made Jake's heart jump in his chest. It caused him to exhale sharply.

"Thank you, Mr. Jenkins. You've been most kind."

Jake nodded and tipped his hat to her. "Miss Howard." He dragged his eyes from hers and forced himself to walk out of the room.

Strolling out into the sunshine, Jake took a deep breath and calmed himself, shook his head and tried to push the image of those eyes from his mind.

Five

Elsie looked up at her son and smiled. "You seem far away, Son."

His cheeks reddened and he ran his fingers through his hair. "Um.. yeah... Um sorry. I just have a lot on my mind."

"Oh?" She sipped at her coffee.

"It's nothing, Ma. I'm sorry. What were you saying?"

"Nothing important. I was just saying that Vi and Jarr are coming for supper tomorrow night."

Jake nodded. "I can't believe they've been married two months already."

"Yes." A light shone in her eyes. "I can't wait to have grandchildren." A loud sigh came from the man seated opposite her. Elsie reached across to squeeze his hand. "I know what you're thinking, Son. It'll happen for you."

He shrugged. "I'm not so sure." But he smiled without meaning to, as a set of amazing mismatched eyes flashed into his mind unexpectedly. He quickly buried that thought. Elsie caught his slight smile and the glimmer of light in his eyes. She said nothing but hope grew in her that her son was beginning to feel happy again.

Jake glanced at the clock. "I better get out on the range, Ma." He stood and put his plate on the counter top.

Elsie stood and followed with her own plate. She placed it down and reached for her apron. Jake wandered over and bent down to kiss her cheek. "I'll see you for supper, Ma."

"Okay, Son."

*   *   *   *

Jake stared absent-mindedly at the herd. His mind wandering to the young lady he'd met the previous day. He'd never before seen a person with two different-colored eyes and they were mesmerising. Not to mention the smell of her perfume. It made his head swirl. "Pull yourself together, Jake, you know nothing about that woman." He sighed. He wasn't free of Chrissy, and his heart was a long way from healed. Nevertheless, he had to admit he'd found Miss Howard intriguing. "It's just her looks," he said aloud. "Any man would notice a woman like that." He sighed.

He didn't hear his brother approach and jerked his head up as Jarrod rode in front of him.

"Hi, Brother. You were far away, I been callin' out to you for a time."

Jake shrugged. "Sorry, just got lots on my mind." His cheeks colored.

Jarrod raised his brows and nodded. He gave his brother a wry smile. "I see. Well, well. Who is she?"

"Don't be ridiculous." Jake scowled.

But Jarrod wasn't convinced. He merely nodded again and opted to change the subject. "You going to the dance?"

"Yeah, I thought I'd take Ma, it's been a while since she's been out."

"Good for you, Jake."

He shrugged. "Ain't got anyone else to take." But a slight flicker of light grew in his eyes as a picture of him twirling Miss Howard around the dance floor flashed into his mind.

Jarrod nodded knowingly. "Well I'm on next watch, you go on home, Charlie and I will watch the herd."

"Thanks. I need to go into town to get a haircut and a shave."

Jarrod tilted his head. "That's a bit over the top for just taking Ma. You hoping to run into a young lady at the dance?"

Jake's eyes twinkled again, but he worked hard to control his facial features, unsuccessfully. "Nah, just thought it wouldn't hurt. It's been a while since I had my hair cut, Ma called me a long-haired lout this morning, I guess it's overdue." He chuckled.

Jarrod nodded. Their mother had a plethora of interesting sayings. "Alright, see you at the dance."

"See you tomorrow night." Jake gave his brother a nod and galloped home.

* * * *

"Evening, Ma." Jake walked in with a wide smile and his hands behind his back.

"Evening, Son, ya hair looks good. You're a handsome lad, just like ya pa."

"Thanks, Ma." He grinned.

Elsie squinted at him. "You look like the cat that got the milk. What's up with you?"

"I wanted to ask you a question."

She tilted her head and frowned. "Oh?"

He lifted his hands from behind his back and presented her with a handful of wildflowers. "These are for you."

Elsie smiled, wiped her hands on her apron and reached for them. "Thank you, Son, that's most kind of you. What's this in aid of?" She buried her nose in the flowers.

"I was wondering if you'd do me the honor of going to the dance with me?"

Elsie grinned. "I'd be delighted. Thank you, Jake, it'll be nice to go with a handsome lad like you." She stepped up on her toes to kiss his clean-shaven cheek.

Jake winked at her. "That's the best news I've had all day."

Elsie chuckled. "Go and wash up. Supper'll be ready soon."

"Yes, Ma'am." He skipped out as Elsie reached for a vase and slipped her flowers in, shaking her head at her thoughtful son.

*   *   *   *

"You scrub up alright." Eli teased his friend as he approached with Sylvia on his arm.

"He's right handsome." Mrs. Jenkins squeezed her son's arm.

"Thanks, Ma."

"I mean it, Son. You look just like yer pa when we were courting. He was the handsomest man in town."

Jake smiled and kissed his ma's hair. "Thanks M..." His voice petered out with a funny little squeak as he noticed Miss Howard walk in. She wore her red hair long and it shimmered in the lamplight. Her ivory dress sparkled with hundreds of shiny navy beads. He swallowed and pressed his lips together lest his mouth gape open. His cheeks reddened. Though he tried, he was unsuccessful at keeping the intrigue from his eyes.

His mother and friend squinted at him and turned to look at the young woman. Mrs. Jenkins grinned at Eli, and he smiled back and nodded.

Jake was oblivious to the well-dressed man who accompanied Lydia Howard. When at last he broke his gaze from her face, he noticed her companion and frowned. His heart sank and he sighed without meaning to.

The man held onto Lydia tightly, his arm around her waist possessively. He led her across to a chair and seated her, then walked over to the beverage stand to talk to some of the other men.

As though propelled by some force outside of himself, Jake found himself walking toward her. There was something about her that drew him. Eli and Mrs. Jenkins raised their brows and glanced at each other again as they watched Jake float over to the lovely girl.

"Good day, Miss Howard."

"Mr. Jenkins. It's nice to see you." She smiled kindly.

He gulped as those eyes met his. "I trust your ankle has healed?" He scrambled for something to keep his mind from the heat rising in his cheeks. But he didn't tug at the collar he suddenly found very restrictive.

"Yes, thank you."

Jake stood for a time, captivated by the mismatched eyes before him.

"Can I help you?" A terse voice came from behind him. He tore his eyes from her face and pivoted on his heels. The well-dressed man stood scowling at him. He raised his brows to Lydia. "What's going on here?"

Lydia swallowed nervously and Jake noticed a slight quiver of fear wash over her. "Mr. Jenkins was asking about my ankle. He helped me when I hurt myself."

The man scowled at Jake again. "You've asked how she is, now I suggest you move along."

Jake squinted at the man. "I meant no harm, Sir. I was just making sure the lady was okay. It's the gentlemanly thing to do when you see a lady sittin' alone."

"Wyatt, he was only being kind." Lydia dared to challenge him by placing her hand on the sleeve of the expensive suit.

The man's eyes spun to hers and he screwed his face up. "I don't need men to be kind to you. You're my fiancée, you ought to be focused on me alone."

Fiancée. Jake's face fell and his heart sank. It was only then he noticed she was indeed wearing a ring. The level of disappointment he felt surprised him to the fullest. The man, Wyatt, didn't even seem to care about her. His tone was stern and uncaring. Her fearful response made Jake's blood boil. He was raised to take care of women, not scare and scar them.

Wyatt stared at Jake with piercing, almost black eyes, with a scowl on his face until Jake turned to walk back to his mother.

"What was that about?" Eli asked. "Who is that woman?"

Jake tried to keep his voice nonchalant. "Oh, I don't know her, she's new to town. I knocked her down by accident a few days ago and helped her to the clinic. I was just asking her if her ankle had healed. Her fiancé didn't seem to appreciate me being there." He failed to remain nonchalant and Eli caught the disappointment in his friend's tone when he said the word fiancé.

They continued to watch the young woman as Wyatt sat next to her, very close, and wrapped an arm around her. It wasn't the gentle touch of a loving fiancé but the tight grip of a possessive man.

She looked up at Jake briefly, and he saw her tremble slightly. She turned away quickly and continued her conversation with Wyatt.

What does she see in him? Jake shook his head at his own feelings of anger and jealousy. Never had a woman had such a draw on him as she did. He couldn't explain it. He knew absolutely nothing about her, yet he couldn't keep her from his thoughts. He sighed and turned to his mother, attempting to forget about the lovely young woman. She was spoken for, no matter how he felt.

He put his hand out to his mother. "Ma, would you like to dance?"

Elsie grinned at her son and took his hand. "I'd love to, Son."

He winked at his mother and led her to the dancefloor and they took up the waltz.

"You dance well, Jake."

"I should, you taught me." He smiled.

"I taught your pa too." She chuckled. "He wasn't much of a dancer, but he tried for me."

"I like dancing. Chrissy and I enjoyed a whirl on the dancefloor." He sighed.

Elsie squeezed the shoulder she gripped. "It'll happen for you again, Son. There'll be someone else come along."

They fell into the rhythm of the music and followed those around them. Eli spun Sylvia in his arms. Both fixed their eyes on each other. Jake shook his head. "I don't think it'll be long for those two. He seems to really love her."

"Yes, they're well-suited."

"Yes..." Jake's voice trailed off as Wyatt danced past them, with Miss Howard in his arms. He couldn't help but notice the contrast between Eli and Sylvia and the couple before him. The look of love between his friend and his sweetheart was mutual and endearing. But Wyatt's eyes were cold. He held Lydia tight and stiff, his hands resting possessively high on her body. He wasn't leading her so much as pulling her along. Jake could tell her ankle still bothered her and she wasn't up for dancing this evening.

Jake caught Lydia's eyes and his heart lurched, she gave him a sad smile and turned her eyes back to look at Wyatt's chest. The man noticed her look away and scowled at her. He spun them around to turn her away from Jake.

"I'll fetch the gig, Ma, wait inside, it's chilly out now that the sun's down. I'll come for ya when I've got Flick attached to the gig."

Elsie nodded and took a seat near the door to wait. Jake skipped out the door. In the fading twilight, he noticed Wyatt pull up and Miss Howard walk toward the gig. Jake frowned at Wyatt, who stayed on the gig as Lydia attempted to lift her foot up to the step. It was too high for her slight stature and her foot slipped. He hurried over to help. He gently touched her arm. "Would you allow me? Please" His voice was full of compassion.

She nodded, and he put his hands gently on her waist and hoisted her up.

Lydia gave him a shy smile and nodded as she sat on the worn seat next to Wyatt. "Thank you, Mr. Jenkins."

Wyatt scowled at him and thrust an arm around Lydia and slid her close to himself. "Yes. Thank you, Mr. Jenkins." His voice was terse. "Now if ya don't mind, we must git goin'."

Jake stood in stunned silence as they drove away. Miss Howard turned and waved at him as they drove out of the church yard. "Lydia." Wyatt scolded and she snapped her head back to look at the horse before her.

Jake shook his head sadly. *He doesn't deserve her.* He grimaced and hurried over to the corral to fetch Flick.

Elsie concentrated on the horse in front of her. The silence was deafening. "You're awful quiet, Son."

"Yeah, just thinking."

"About the young lady at the dance?"

Jake snapped his head around and looked at her. "Am I that obvious?"

"She's a beautiful girl, I can't blame you for noticing her." She reached over and squeezed his arm. "I'm pleased, Son, it means ya heart is healing."

He sighed. "I'm a long way from ready for a courtship, Ma, and she's spoken for. I was just thinking about the young man she was with. He doesn't seem to even care about her. I can't imagine treating a woman like that, even if she was a stranger." He gritted his teeth and scowled into the semi-darkness.

Elsie smiled. "You're a kind lad, Jake."

"I don't know what she sees in him, it's obvious he doesn't love her."

"There are plenty of reasons women court men, and many have nothing to do with love."

He nodded and they traveled the rest of the distance in silence but Jake's mind was busy. He could see Lydia's mismatched eyes clearly in his mind's eye. Somehow they pierced deep into his heart and he could see them in his dreams. *Funny, Chrissy never affected me that way.* He struggled now to even recall Chrissy's face. He sighed loudly as they pulled into their yard. His mother squeezed his arm sympathetically and vowed to step up her prayers. It was good to see him beginning to feel hope again.

Six

It'd been some time since Jake had been to town, not since the dance. He'd missed two church services in a row, with issues on the ranch keeping him away. But he could no longer put off a trip. He urgently needed more lumber for the next section of fencing to extend the corrals. He hitched the long wagon to Frog and Toad, their quarterhorses.

He jumped on the wagon and clucked to the pair they affectionately called 'The Amphibians.' It'd been a family joke since Jarrod had mixed up equine and amphibian in a school project. It was how the two horses had got their unusual names. Jake chuckled as he recalled it, and turned the amphibians toward town.

He sighed and smiled into the air. Jarrod and Vi had given him the news the previous night that he'd be an uncle sometime in the new year. He was delighted for his brother, but it was bittersweet. He couldn't help but think that he and Chrissy could well have had a family by now. He sighed. It'd been almost two years since she left. He knew the chances of ever seeing her again were slim to none and, no doubt wherever she was, she'd moved on and found herself a new life.

I wish I could move on. He shook his head. The closest he'd come to thinking of another woman was Miss Howard. Every time he saw her he felt drawn to her. He shrugged it off, for what else could he do?

"There is nothing I can do about her. She's spoken for." No matter how he felt about her, it wasn't right to have feelings for someone else's girl, so he buried those thoughts as deep as he could. Still, he could see her eyes in his mind every time he closed his.

He groaned and forced his mind back to focus on the tasks of the day as he plodded toward town. His thoughts were interrupted as he entered the outskirts of town by a sound like whimpering. Coming around the corner toward the lumber mill he noticed a woman picking blueberries, sniffing away tears and trying to stifle sobs. "Ohhh." His heart flipped as he saw the red hair. He pulled the amphibians to a stop and jumped down. Flicking the reins over a shrub, he hurried over to her.

"Miss Howard? Are you alright?"

Lydia spun on her heels to look at him and swiped hastily at the tears on her cheeks. "Yes. Ohh. Ummm. Mr. Jenkins," she stammered. "Thank you. I'm quite alright, truly." She gave him a shaky smile.

Jake put one hand on her arm. "Forgive me, Miss but you don't look alright. Is there something I can do to help?" He couldn't help but have compassion for her.

Lydia's lips trembled. "No, I don't think so."

"May I ask what's upset you, please? I'm a good listener."

She smiled and nodded her head. His kindness put her at ease. He gestured to a small clearing nearby and removed his coat. He lay it on the ground and gestured for her to sit. Taking a seat opposite her, he placed his hat down next to him.

"I'm sorry, I'm just being silly really." The sadness in her mismatched eyes cut him deeply. "I had a disagreement with Wyatt this morning, and I guess I'm feeling sorry for myself."

"I'm sorry." Jake didn't know what else to say. He touched her shoulder kindly. "Is there anything I can help with?" He chided himself for his forwardness, he couldn't help it; this woman was so intriguing. He dropped his hand. "I'm sorry, you only have to tell me what you want to tell me. It isn't my business."

Strangely she felt comfortable with Jake. She'd not seen him but a few times in town, but when he'd carried her to the clinic, she'd seen a gentleness and a kindness in him. Wyatt never treated her like that. He never wanted to listen or cared about any of the things she liked. He'd only dropped her off at the berry patch because she'd promised him pie.

Lydia shrugged and lifted those intriguing eyes to Jake's. He groaned internally and fought the urge to take her in his arms and kiss her soft lips. His head began to spin.

She gave him a sad smile and sighed. "It's nothing really, we just argued about our wedding is all. I can't get Wyatt to pin down a date."

"Really? I should think he'd want to marry you as soon as possible." The words were out before he could stop them. He bit his lip to keep himself from saying more. *How could he put her off. I'd marry her in a heartbeat.* Jake sucked in a breath, where did that thought come from? He didn't even know this woman.

"Wyatt isn't really the romantic type." Lydia lowered her head. "I'm sorry. I shouldn't speak badly of him. That's not right."

Jake touched her arm gently. "It's okay, whatever you say I'll keep it to myself."

She nodded and smiled.

He pulled his hand back and changed the subject. "Can I ask what brought you to Hopes Brook?"

Lydia nodded. "Wyatt got a job at the bank, so I applied for the school and I'll be starting in September."

"You're a teacher?" Why did that thrill him so much?

"Well, I will be; this is my first school. I just graduated in June."

"Where did you study?"

"Minneapolis."

Jake nodded. "Are you from there?" He found himself eager to know everything about this intriguing woman.

"No. I'm from Virginia originally. Since we're to be married, I followed Wyatt to college and then out here. I guess it was really the Lord who led us here."

"How did you and Wyatt meet?" Jake couldn't believe he was asking these questions. They seemed to be coming from outside of himself.

"It's a bit of a story." She gave him a shaky smile. "I was raised with his family for a time."

He raised his brows, encouraging her to continue.

Lydia smiled. "My mother died in childbirth so my father raised my older brother and me with my grandmother's help. Pa was killed in the war and Wyatt's father, Sergeant Colin McCain was my father's best friend. Pa made him promise if anything happened to him, he'd take in Arty and me. So when Grandmother died, we were taken to live with the McCains. I was eight and Arty was twelve the same age as Wyatt. Uncle Colin and Aunt Gloria took care of us. They weren't overly nurturing, but they were kind. Aunt Glo died when I was fifteen and Arty had already left home. He's in the navy and he and his wife live in Virginia. When I decided I wanted to be a teacher, Uncle Colin agreed to pay on the proviso that I agreed to marry Wyatt. Evidently he'd told his father that he wanted me." She shrugged and blushed slightly.

Jake frowned. He'd wondered how such a lovely girl had ended up with a man like him. He merely nodded and waited for her to continue. He was not entirely able to keep the grimace off his face.

"I know what you're thinking. Wyatt isn't the most romantic type, but his family was good to me and I feel like I owe them." She shrugged. "And Pa loved Uncle Colin. I have his diary and he wrote a lot about their time together in the war. I owe it to Pa to pay back their kindness. Wyatt's not a horrible man and I know he'll provide for me." She smiled sadly. "I'm not sure when we'll get married. Every time I broach the subject Wyatt just shrugs and says, "When I'm ready." It's what we were arguing about this morning.

45

I'm living in the cramped boarding house while he lives in the cabin he purchased. I go every morning to make him breakfast and I take care of the house for him even though I don't live there. I told him since I was basically there all the time anyway we ought to marry so I could move in. He said he'd marry when he's good and ready." She frowned. "I don't know why I'm telling you all this." She blushed and hung her head.

Jake reached across and touched her arm. "I'll keep it to myself, you have my word." Internally he seethed, that man did not deserve a sweet girl like her. He couldn't help but get lost in her eyes again.

"Thank you for listening, Mr. Jenkins, you're most kind. I'm sorry for taking up your time."

"That's okay, Miss Howard. I couldn't leave you there upset like that."

"I'm okay now, I guess I just feel a little lonesome sometimes."

"I can understand that. You can be in a crowd of people and still feel alone."

"I think the hardest thing is that Wyatt doesn't share my faith. I wish we could open the Bible together. It saddens me to think of spending my life with a man who won't be the Christian leader I need him to be."

"You don't have to marry him, you know." The words were out before Jake could stop them. "I'm sorry." He grimaced.

Lydia hung her head. "Yes I do. I owe his family and..." She shrugged and raised sad eyes to him.

"Besides, where else would I go? I don't have any money. Wyatt pays for my board and expenses. What else can a woman with no family and no means do?"

Jake closed his eyes and sighed. "I'm sorry." He grimaced. Her situation made him sad. He couldn't imagine being trapped in a loveless marriage. He'd commit Lydia to prayer and hope that God would see fit to free her from this man.

Lydia shrugged and gave him a sideways smile. "Don't be sorry, it could be so much worse. I have my faith and the Lord sustains me. I don't know where I'd be without Him. And if it weren't for the McCain family, I shudder to think what would've become of me. There aren't many opportunities for single women of no means in the city. Marrying Wyatt is better than the alternative." She smiled but her eyes betrayed her true feelings.

He nodded and gave her a supportive smile, what else could he do?

Lydia changed the subject. "Have you always lived in the Dakota territories, Mr. Jenkins?"

Jake smiled and shook his head. "No, we lived in Missouri until I was six. Pa had the mercantile there but had a hankering to go ranching. His best friend Charlie and he moved out here, and Charlie took over as foreman. He's still our foreman, but my brother and I own the ranch together, since Pa died."

Lydia's eyes filled with tears. "I'm sorry."

Jake was touched by her compassion. "He died when I was fifteen. We'd been working the ranch since we were boys so Charlie taught Jarrod and me the running of the place."

"Is Jarrod your brother?"

"Yep, he's a year younger than me."

"Is it just the two of you?" Lydia found herself drawn to Jake, he was so easy to talk to. *I never feel like I can speak to Wyatt so freely like this.*

"Yes." He grimaced. "Ma had a little girl shortly after we arrived, but she was stillborn."

Lydia's face curled up and she squeezed his arm. "Ohhh, I'm sorry."

Jake nodded and gave her a sad smile. "It's okay, Georgina's buried with my father. We like to think they're together in Glory."

"Oh, they are, and I believe they're watching over us."

"I think so too."

"May I ask? Do you have a sweetheart?" Lydia bit her lip and blushed. "I'm sorry, Mr. Jenkins. My mouth runs away with me sometimes. You don't have to answer that."

He screwed up his mouth and sighed. "I was engaged once."

"Oh." Lydia didn't know what else to say. "Did she pass?"

Jake looked up at her and managed a shy smile. "No. Chrissy left town, she witnessed a crime and the Marshalls took her away for her protection a little under two years ago." He shrugged. "I don't know where she is."

Lydia's mouth dropped open, and she gripped his arm again. "I'm sorry."

A horse and gig rode up and Wyatt jumped down and strutted toward them. "What's this? You two look awfully cozy." He scowled.

Lydia's face drained of all color, she snatched her arm back abruptly. "Mr. Jenkins stopped to see if I was okay. He was just being kind."

Wyatt fixed dark eyes on Jake and sneered. "Yes, he's often being kind. I thought you were picking berries, not sitting out here flirting with another man. I've told you how I feel about that." He reached down and roughly hauled Lydia to her feet. A slight whimper escaped her and her eyes flooded with unshed tears.

Jake leaped to his feet. "Hey, don't treat her like that."

Wyatt spun on his heels and stared daggers at him. "What's it got to do with you? She ain't your girl. I recommend you mind yer own business and stay away." He shoved Lydia toward his gig and took a step toward Jake, standing at his full height. He was shorter and thinner than the rancher and wasn't remotely intimidating.

Jake crossed his arms over his chest. "I'll never stand by and say nothing when a woman is being mistreated." He scowled at Wyatt and gripped him in his steely glare.

Wyatt's eyes grew wide and he stepped forward. "Mistreated? What's it to do with you how I treat my wife?"

"She isn't your wife."

"She's betrothed to me and it's got nothing to do with you, Mr. Jenkins." He poked Jake in the chest.

Jake merely raised his brows and fought every instinct to hit the man in the chin.

"Wyatt, please don't. I'll come with you, you don't need to get angry, Mr. Jenkins was just being friendly."

Wyatt pivoted on his heels and sneered at her. "I'll tell you who you can and can't be friendly with."

"You can't stop me having friends, Wyatt," Lydia said in a small voice, afraid to defy him.

Wyatt scowled and covered the distance between them. He sneered at her and hissed through his teeth, "Yes, I can, and you won't see this man again. Do you hear me?"

"I can't promise that. I'll see him at church sometimes, and we live in the same town." Her lips trembled.

Wyatt gripped her chin roughly. "Then perhaps you ought not to be going to that church."

"Leave her alone." Jake seethed, Lydia's mismatched eyes were full of fear. He stepped toward them, ready to defend her.

Wyatt dropped his hand and turned to look at Jake. "Stay out of it. This isn't your business, what I do with my woman."

"You ought to treat her with respect."

Wyatt flashed him a smarmy smile. "You'll never get a woman to obey ya, if you're gonna be soft like that, no wonder you ain't got a woman."

"Wyatt, please, can't you just take me home?" Lydia pleaded.

Wyatt sneered and lifted his hand as though he was going to strike her. Terror filled her eyes, and she shrunk back from him. He lowered his hand. "Get on the gig."

She nodded and hoisted herself up to wait on the seat. Wyatt turned to Jake who still stood with his arms crossed, and a furrowed brow.

"Stay away from my woman." Wyatt thrust a finger out at him and pursed his lips, then climbed up on the gig beside Lydia. Holding her tightly against himself, he flicked the rein and galloped away. Jake was certain he heard a whimper from Lydia as they galloped off.

"Lord, protect her," he said aloud and wiped away a tear. He couldn't fathom a man ever treating a woman that way. "He doesn't deserve her, Lord." A protectiveness and compassion filled him. If there was anything he could do to get her out of that engagement, he would.

Reluctantly he picked up his coat, thrust it over his shoulders and climbed back up on the wagon, flicked the reins at the amphibians and headed off to town, praying without ceasing for Lydia.

Seven

Jake paced back and forth on the porch. Elsie walked out with two cups of hot coffee. She sat down in one of the chairs and put the cups on the table between them. "What's got up your nose, Son?"

He stopped pacing and flicked his hair off his face. "What makes you think something's wrong?"

"I'm your mother. I can tell when something's eating you. Sit, drink your coffee and talk to me."

He thrust himself into the chair, and grabbed the coffee cup, sploshing some hot liquid over the side and onto his hand. He cringed and took a long draft; the coffee burned on the way down, but it was strangely soothing. He took a deep breath and exhaled loudly.

"Girl trouble?"

"Nah, she ain't my girl." He sighed loudly and grimaced.

"You mean Miss Howard?"

"Yeah."

"Do you love her?"

Jake flicked his head around and squinted. "No, she's spoken for, that wouldn't be right."

"But you like her?"

He smiled without meaning to. "She's interesting. is all. She has the most amazing eyes. We talked today. She's got a sad story, but she's strong and brave. But I'd never get in the way of someone else's relationship." He sighed sharply. *More's the pity, he doesn't deserve her. She's a sweet girl, and she deserves to be treated gently.* He had to confess if she wasn't betrothed to Wyatt McCain, he'd love to get to know her. It was more than her eyes. There was something about her. He wasn't yet free of Chrissy but if anyone could replace her in his heart, it would be Lydia Howard. *Pull yourself together, Jake, she's spoken for and that's that.*

"So, what's got you so angry?"

Jake drained his cup and thrust it down on the table forcefully. His mother frowned and grimaced, hoping it wouldn't break. "It's him. He doesn't deserve her."

Elsie raised her brows. "Why?"

"He's cruel to her. No woman should be treated that way."

"Why does she stay with him?"

"She told me she feels obliged because his family took her in when her father died. He's got her so beat down I think she feels that she can't do any better."

"But you think she could?" Elsie tipped her head to the side.

"Ma, I know what you're thinking, but she's betrothed to another man and unless that changes, there's nothing I can do about it."

"I know, Son. Perhaps you'll have to make her see what she's missing and she may change her mind about him."

"I dunno. He's got a hold over her. She depends on him for all her expenses."

"They aren't married though, are they?"

"No, apparently he's reluctant to set a date."

53

"I can't imagine why, if what you say is true it sounds like he'd like her to look after him."

"I think he's doing it deliberately to show her he's in control. I can't imagine ever treating a woman like that."

"You're a good man, and you'll make someone an excellent husband someday."

Jake sighed. "I'm not holding my breath."

"You're still a young man, not yet twenty-four years old."

He shrugged. "I know but I'm not sure it'll ever happen. The woman I loved left, and now a woman I could love isn't available. Perhaps I'll just be alone."

"Just because two women haven't worked out doesn't mean no one will."

Jake thrust his arms over his chest. "There aren't very many available girls in this town, Ma. It's not like they're lining up."

"You could send for a bride."

Jake's head snapped up and he squinted at his mother. "What are you talking about?"

"I know men who've ordered a mail-order bride and been very happy."

He screwed up his face. "No, I couldn't. I think these things happen in God's timing; they shouldn't be forced like that."

Elsie reached across and gripped his arm. "It's better than being alone; perhaps it's the way God wants to bring along your wife."

"I dunno, Ma. Perhaps I'm not meant to have a wife. Perhaps I have nothing to offer a woman."

"Jacob James Jenkins, you're a catch. You're handsome and strong, you're half owner of the biggest ranch in these parts and you're a good, kind Christian man, you have everything to offer."

He smiled. "Thanks, Ma. I'd die a lucky man to have even half of what you and Pa had."

She squeezed his arm gently. "I'm praying for you, Son. I can't wait to see you as a husband and father. You'll be a good one."

"Thanks for your faith in me, Ma, and thanks for raising me to know the Lord. It saddens me to hear Lydi..." he caught himself. "Miss Howard say that the man she's going to marry doesn't share her faith. I can think of nothing more wonderful than serving the Lord alongside a woman. I envy Jarr."

Elsie nodded and patted his arm. There was nothing more to say.

* * * *

"Hello, Ma. What brings you here?" Viola stroked her rounding abdomen as she welcomed Elsie in.

"I need your help with something if you don't mind?"

"Certainly, if I can. Would you like a cup of coffee?"

"Yes, thank you."

Viola nodded and gestured to the living room. Elsie sat down and looked around while she waited. Viola and Jarrod had done a nice job making the small cabin their own. Chrissy's taste had being wildly different. Viola had filled the home with bright pillows, curtains and rugs. It was cosy and charming. She was a bubbly, vivacious girl and the house expressed it. Chrissy had preferred lighter, plainer colors and matched up every room.

Viola was soon back. She placed two cups of coffee and a plate of cookies on the table between the armchairs and sat down. "Now, what can I help with, Ma?"

"Do you have the most recent newspaper?"

"Yes, of course. Do you not have one at the house?"

"Yes I do, but I want to keep this a secret from Jake."

"Oh?"

"I want to check the mail-order bride advertisements."

Viola raised her brows. "You want to get a stranger here for him to marry?"

Elsie shrugged. "I just don't like to see him so down. I know he wants a family someday."

"Are you sure that's a good idea? He might not be happy about us meddling."

"Not if he doesn't know she's a mail-order bride. What if she just moved to town and he could get to know her?"

"What if he doesn't love her?"

"I guess we'd have to cross that bridge when we come to it."

"Ma, it wouldn't be fair to lure her to town under false pretences."

Elsie sighed. "You're right, I suppose. I just hate to see him hurting."

Vi smiled. "We'll just have to step up the prayers. God is the ultimate matchmaker."

"Yes, you're right, Dear, of course. I should know better than to meddle with God's plans."

"You're just being a mother." Viola rubbed her abdomen. "Loving her son. I think I'd feel the same."

Elsie smiled. "How's the sickness?"

"It's bearable, I feel much better than last week, and Jarrod's very attentive to me."

"He'd better be. I didn't raise him to be unkind."

"He's certainly not that, Ma. He's the kindest man I know."

"Lucky for some."

Viola frowned and tilted her head in question.

"Oh, a young lady in town is being badly treated by the man she's betrothed to. Jake has witnessed it more than once and it's had quite an effect on him. He feels bad for her."

"He's a kind man, too. It breaks my heart that Chrissy left him."

"I don't believe she had a choice."

"Do you think she'll ever come back?"

"I don't know. As far as I know the crooks are still at large. It's been two years; she'll have moved on by now."

"Quite possibly. I'll step up my prayers for Jake. Jarr and I pray for him every day. He can't bear to see his brother unhappy. He was supposed to be married long before Jarrod."

"Yes, we never imagined Jarrod would ever settle down." Elsie reached across and squeezed her daughter-in-law's arm. "I guess it just took the right woman."

Viola smiled. "I guess so, and Jake will find her too. We'll just keep on praying."

Eight

"So how's it going with Sylvia?" Jake fell into step with his friend as they headed toward the café.

Eli grinned. "She's a heck of a woman."

Jake slapped Eli on the back. "You've got it bad."

"I've got it good, my friend. I can see why you were so sappy when you got engaged."

Jake closed his eyes and sighed.

Eli grimaced. "I'm sorry. I don't mean to drag up old memories."

"It's okay, I guess I just feel a bit like I'm being left behind. We should've been married almost two years, could've had a family by now."

Eli gripped his shoulder and they paused on the boardwalk outside the café. "I'm sorry. I shouldn't flaunt my happiness in front of you."

"No, it's fine, you deserve to be happy. Perhaps I can just live vicariously through you." Jake gave his friend a genuine smile as he pushed open the door. "I'm serious, my friend. I'm happy for you. Are you making plans?"

They took their seat at the table and caught Hannah-Mae's eye. She lifted the coffeepot to them and they nodded their thank you.

Jake tilted his head and thrust his hands across his chest, his question still hanging in the air.

Eli shrugged and then grinned broadly. He put his hand in his pocket, pulled out a small box, and slid it across the table.

Jake squinted and lifted the box, opened it and shook his head. He slid it back. "When do you plan to propose?"

"I've still gotta talk to her pa. I'm trying to pluck up the courage."

"What's the hesitation?"

"She's the pastor's daughter. I'm worried I'm not good enough for his girl."

"You asked him if you could court, didn't you?"

"Yeah."

"Well, I'm sure he's expecting you'll propose sooner or later. Isn't that usually the intention when you court? Or at least it's not really a surprise."

"He's always been very welcoming."

"He loves you, Eli. You're like a son to him."

Eli nodded. "He's said as much to me a few times."

"So talk to Pastor Moore. I don't understand your hesitation."

"Sylvia's his only child. He lost his wife a few years ago. I worry that he's gonna struggle to lose her."

"He won't be losing her; he'll be gaining a son. He'll be delighted. You're a good man and he's been happy to have you court his daughter so he must like you."

Eli nodded and smiled.

Jake raised his brows again and drained his cup.

Eli grinned widely. "I'll talk to him tonight."

"Attaboy. You won't regret it." A wistful look crossed Jake's face.

"Do you?"

"Regret getting engaged to Chrissy?"

Eli nodded.

"Not at all. I regret how it turned out, but I loved her."

"Do you still?"

Jake shrugged. "It's fading. I guess when you know the person is gone, then there's no point keeping the flame alive." A blush crossed his cheeks.

Eli caught it and squinted at his friend. "There's a twinkle in your eye. Is there someone else on your mind?" He raised his brows knowingly.

Jake tried hard to remain nonchalant but he couldn't keep his cheeks from reddening. He shrugged. "Even if there was, she's off limits."

"Miss Howard?"

"She's with McCain. It's wrong to feel something for someone else's girl." Jake shrugged and sighed.

"But you do feel something for her?"

Jake looked around to make sure no one was listening. The café wasn't very full and they were alone in their corner. He nodded. "Can't help it, I feel drawn to her somehow. It's just her looks I imagine and I feel compassion for her."

"That's all?"

"It's all it can ever be!" Jake shrugged and ran his fingers through his hair. "What choice do I have?"

Eli shook his head. "I guess you can be there for her as a friend."

"I'm not sure that's a good idea, every time I've been around her, he's made it clear I'm not welcome. It makes me so angry. He treats her unkindly. I ran into her a few days ago and she was upset by him. I watched him manhandle her. He views her as little more than property." Jake clenched his teeth.

Eli shuddered. "I can't imagine that." The bank clock struck the hour and both men stood. "I better get back to work."

"Me too. All the best with the pastor, I'll be praying for you."

"Thanks, Friend." Eli pushed open the door and they strolled out into the sunshine. "I'll be praying for you too, as always."

"I'm sure in need of it."

"Huh, aren't we all?"

The two men nodded to each other and hurried away.

*   *   *   *

"Where are you off to so early in the morning?" Jarrod asked as he rode out toward the range and passed his brother heading toward town on the saddle horse.

"Got a few errands to run."

Jarrod noticed a slight blush to his brother's cheeks and the hint of a sparkle in his eyes. He raised his brows and nodded. "School starts today, doesn't it?"

Jake gulped and swallowed. "I wouldn't know." He shrugged and his face reddened.

Jarrod nodded and reached across to grip his brother's shoulder. "Be careful, Jake. Don't set yourself up for heartbreak."

Jake returned his nod, sighing loudly. "I know. I just find myself so drawn to her. I'll never pursue anything though; that would be wrong."

"Then what do you hope to achieve?"

"I dunno, Jarr. I just know I'm tired of being alone and I feel like God has brought her into my life for a reason."

Jarrod grimaced. "Jake, you can't go there. She's engaged to another man, no matter how you feel about her. God would never honor that."

"Doesn't mean I can't be her friend."

Jarrod shook his head. "That's not a good idea and you know it."

Jake sighed loudly. "It's all very well for you, Jarr. You've got your happily ever after."

"And you will too, but this isn't the way."

"I know what I'm doing."

"I hope you do, Brother." Jarrod's creased brow showed he was certain he knew the futility of his brother's actions.

"I do." Jake clucked to Duke and galloped away.

Jarrod paused and watched him go. "Oh no. Lord, I pray you'll keep him from doing something he'll later regret. Keep them both from harm. And bring him happiness." He finished his short prayer and turned toward the range.

*   *   *   *

Jake galloped into town, Jarrod's words rang in his ears. "Lord, I know it's wrong to have feelings for someone else's girl, but he doesn't deserve her." He sighed loudly. "But that doesn't make it right." He pulled Duke to a slow walk and decided he'd visit Eli instead, to find out how his talk with the pastor went. He chuckled as he thought about his friend. He was genuinely happy for Eli and Sylvia.

As he rounded the corner, he noticed Miss Howard walking toward the schoolhouse, with her basket over her arm and three books wedged under her other arm. Jake hurried over to her and dismounted. "Good morning, Miss Howard."

She stopped walking and smiled. "Mr. Jenkins."

He linked his arm through Duke's rein, and they fell into step. "Will you allow me to carry that for you?"

"I can manage."

"I don't doubt that, Miss Howard, but it's the polite thing for a gentleman to do for a lady."

She smiled at him and her mismatched eyes shone. "Very well, that's most kind." She passed over her books and basket.

"So, it's your first day?"

"Yes." Her face lit up. "I'm so excited." Lydia clutched her hands together. The passion in her eyes was obvious.

"How many students will you have?" *See this is fine, we can chat casually without it meaning anything.* He attempted to convince himself.

"Fifteen to begin with." She grimaced. "I'm not sure I'm worthy of the task."

"You'll be wonderful, I'm sure."

Lydia blushed. "Thank you."

He stopped at the school house stairs and passed her over her books and basket.

"Thank you, Mr. Jenkins."

"You're most welcome. All the best for your first day."

"I thank you."

He fixed his eyes on hers again and it made him gasp. *Jake you can't let yourself fall in love with her.* But no matter how hard he tried, those eyes called to him and her full lips begged him to kiss them. He took a deep breath and buried the feelings as deep as he could. He nodded to her and hurried away before he said or did anything he regretted.

He sighed loudly. "Help me, Lord, Jarr was right, I can't do this. It's not fair on any of us." He shook his head and turned to walk toward town.

Jake rode into the livery and dismounted. "Eli?"

Eli stood up from the stall he was mucking out, leaned his pitchfork against the wall and walked out. He swiped his forearm across his brow. "Jake." He nodded to his friend, unable to keep the wide grin off his face or the sparkle from his eyes.

Jake raised his brows and leaned back against an empty stall. "I know that goofy grin. I take it things went well with the pastor?"

"I hope you aren't busy October first."

Jake tilted his head to side.

Eli gripped his shoulder. "I'll be needing a best man."

"What are you saying?"

"I'm engaged, my friend."

Jake nodded and slapped his friend on the back. "Congratulations." The two men embraced. "I'm thrilled for you." A slight wobble to his voice betrayed the bittersweetness of the occasion for Jake.

"Thanks, Jake. You're my best friend and I want you up there with me."

"I'll be there."

Eli frowned then. "What brings you into town this morning?"

Jake shrugged one shoulder. "Nothing really, I just wanted to know how you'd got on."

Eli squinted and pursed his lips. "And school started today?"

Jake sighed, shook his head, and leaned back against the stall again. "Yeah."

"I'm sorry, Friend. It doesn't seem fair."

"Fair?"

"First the love of your life leaves, then an amazing woman turns up, one you could love, and she's with him."

Jake nodded and thrust his arms over his chest. "Yeah."

"You can't pursue anything with her."

"I know."

"So what are you hoping will happen?"

"I'm hoping she'll see him for who he really is and be free of him."

"So she can be with you?"

"I admit that would be great, but more than I want to be with her, I want her to be happy and he does not make her happy."

"So, what if they part, but you don't end up with her?"

"Then I'll just be relieved she's not with him. Her happiness is all that matters."

"If it's any consolation, I'm praying for you. I want you to be happy too. Miss Howard or otherwise."

"Thanks, you're a good friend, Eli."

"Anytime."

"Well, I'll leave you to it. I best get back to the ranch."

Eli nodded.

Jake paused at the door. "Congratulations my friend. Sylvia's a good woman."

"I think so." Eli's grin was so wide his cheeks hurt.

Jake shook his head, mounted his horse, and galloped back to the ranch.

Nine

Jake leaned back against the tree and stretched his long legs out in front of him. He looked over the common at all the children, running and playing, the families sitting on blankets enjoying their lunch. He smiled and sighed longingly.

"You okay, Jake?"

He looked up at his sister-in-law as Jarrod helped her sit down on the blanket. "Yeah, just feeling a bit nostalgic."

Vi gripped his arm and Jarrod took a seat next to his mother. "I understand. We're praying for you."

"Thank you. You should all save your pity; I'm fine."

"It's not pity, Jake. We just want to see you happy."

Jake nodded at his brother and gave him a sad smile. His mother passed him a plate of pie and he winked at her.

"Maybe you should take Ma up on her offer."

Jake swallowed his mouthful and snapped his head up at his brother, his brows creased in question.

"Get a mail-order bride."

Elise gasped and busied herself pouring coffee for everyone.

Jake turned his head to look at his mother. "You've been talking about this?"

"Son, I just want you to be happy."

Jake sighed loudly. "I wish you'd all just leave me alone on this." He put the plate down, stood up and strode away. He caught Miss Howard's eye as he walked past. She sat on a plaid picnic blanket with several of her students chatting around her. The joy on her face made his heart sick. The only consolation was that Wyatt wasn't there. But then of course he wouldn't be, he never attended church or town events. Jake closed his eyes, hung his head and hurried away. He passed the blanket closest to the church and Eli leaped up. "Jake?"

Jake stopped walking but didn't turn around. Eli nodded to Sylvia and walked around in front of Jake. "You okay?"

"I've just had enough of everyone's pity." Jake sighed loudly.

Eli raised his brows, no question was needed.

Jake closed his eyes. "Everyone's trying to run my life. Ma wants to get me a mail-order bride."

"Would that be such a bad thing?"

Jake scowled at his friend. "You don't think I can work this out on my own either?"

"I never said that. I know men who've got mail-order brides and been very happy."

"I couldn't marry someone I didn't love."

"How do you know you wouldn't love them over time?"

Jake sighed. "My heart is already spoken for," he admitted aloud.

Eli nodded. "Chrissy's gone, you have to accept that."

"Wasn't talking about Chrissy," Jake mumbled under his breath and lowered his eyes.

Eli's brows flew up. "Miss Howard?"

Jake sighed loudly.

"Jake."

Eli's tone made Jake's head snap up. "What?"

"You can't fall in love with someone else's girl. I'm sorry you're feeling lonesome, but it's wrong."

Jake sighed loudly again. "I know, but my heart might take some convincing." He turned sad eyes to the lovely teacher sitting under the tree, laughing with her students. The way her face lit up made his heart lurch.

Eli gripped his shoulder. "Jake, you gotta find a way to get over her. She's not available, and that's that."

"It's not fair." Jake's voice trembled.

Eli nodded. "I know. You're right, it isn't fair and I'm sorry. I really am."

"It's not your fault. I just gotta work this out. I gotta watch her with that jerk and it makes my heart ache. Whenever I see her, all I want to do is take her in my arms and kiss her. I see her in my mind when I close my eyes. It's like she's buried deep in my soul and I can't seem to get her out."

Eli nodded again, somewhat lost for words in how to help his lovelorn friend.

"If he was at least a good man who made her happy, I could accept it."

Eli gave him a smirk.

"Okay, at least I could tolerate it more than I can now. Watching her with him is awful. Whenever I see them together, I want to punch his lights out."

"That won't achieve anything."

"I know."

"So, what're you going to do?"

Jake ran his fingers through his hair. "Stay away I guess."

"Wha'd'ya mean?"

"We're mostly self-sufficient on the ranch; I could stay away from town easy enough. Ma and Jarr can go to town when needed."

"You can't shut yourself away; that won't change anything."

Jake sniffed away his emotions and raised his hands in the air and shoved them in his pockets. "What do you suggest I do?" His face screwed up in agony.

"I don't know. I'm sorry, Jake. I don't know what to say to help you. I want to, trust me. If I could change this for you, I would, in a heartbeat. Sylv and I have been praying for you non-stop."

"Great, so now someone else knows how pathetic I am." Jake rolled his eyes.

Eli gripped his shoulder again. "You aren't pathetic, Jake, you can't help how you feel."

Jake closed his eyes and sighed again. He'd been doing a lot of that lately. "Thanks for the prayers."

"Of course. You need to talk; you know where I am."

"Thanks." Jake nodded.

"Where're you going?"

"I'm not sure. Thought I might go to the lake and throw a line in. Do some thinking."

"Okay."

"Will you tell Jarr to make sure Ma gets home. I'll find my own way back."

Eli nodded. "Feel free to take the black from the livery."

Jake gave his friend a grateful smile, took one last look at Miss Howard, grimaced, and walked away from the common.

He strode slowly toward the livery with his hands in his pockets. "Lord, I need you to help me with this. I don't know what to do. I can no longer deny that I love Lydia. I know it's wrong." He sighed and entered the livery and reached for a bridle off a hook. Jake paused; he could hear giggling coming from one of the stalls. He frowned and strode over. "What...?" He thrust open the gate. "What?" was all he could manage.

Wyatt McCain sat up and Miss Myrtle Fredrickson pulled her blouse closed and sat up slowly, her cheeks deeply red.

Jake frowned. "Exactly what is going on here?" He scowled at Wyatt.

The man stood up and sneered at Jake. He could see lipstick on the man's face and neck, the same shade as Myrtle's lips.

"I'm waiting for an explanation." Jake frowned.

"I don't owe you an explanation. Ain't none of your business what I do."

"What about Miss Howard?"

Wyatt shrugged. "What about her?"

"Aren't you supposed to be engaged to her?"

"Yeah, so?"

"And you're here..." how did he say the words? "With a saloon girl."

"So, what's your point, Jenkins?"

"You're being unfair to your fiancée."

Wyatt shrugged.

"Don't you have anything to say? How can you treat her like that?"

Wyatt smirked. "What she doesn't know won't hurt her."

"Suppose I tell her."

"You'd like that, wouldn't you. You've been trying to get your hands on her since we came to town."

"I'd treat her better than you do..."

Lydia noticed Eli talking to Jake. The look on Jake's face made her sad. She knew he was hurting, and she felt for him. He was a nice man, he'd been nothing but kind to her and she hoped he might be a friend. She got the impression there was a deep sadness over him. Seeing Jake walk away, she excused herself from the children and walked over to Eli.

"Mr. Jackson." She smiled.

"Miss Howard." He nodded to her. They both paused and a silence fell over them.

"If you'll excuse me, Ma'am. I must get back to my fiancée."

"Wait. Please, is Jake... ah Mr. Jenkins okay? He looked distressed."

"Why do you want to know?" Eli tilted his head to the side.

"I'm not sure. I just feel like he's got a deep sadness over him. I feel bad for him."

"He'll be okay, Ma'am. He's just got a lot on his mind."

"I understand. Do you know where he's going?"

Eli shrugged his shoulders. "Said something about going fishing. I told him he could take a horse, he might be at the livery. I think he just wants to be alone for a time."

"I understand." Lydia smiled at Eli. He nodded to her and walked away. She began to walk back to the blanket but something drew her to search for Jake.

She walked slowly to the livery. "Lord, I know Jake is hurting. Please heal his heart. He's a kind man and he deserves to be happy." She heard voices coming from the livery and paused to listen.

"Pffft. I knew you had a sad crush on her. You're pathetic," Wyatt shouted.

"You don't deserve her."

"What and you do?"

"I'm not saying that. But how can you treat her the way you do?"

"Treat her in what way?"

"You don't care about her, you're not kind to her. You're here with this woman. Who knows what you were doing in here, or what you might've done had I not walked in."

Lydia gasped and put a hand over her mouth. She crept a little closer and continued to listen.

"Wouldn't be the first time." Wyatt smirked.

"What? You've been with other women?"

"So?"

"How can you?"

"Lydia won't give me what I want, so I have to get it somewhere?"

"What do you mean? You aren't married, so you can't expect anything from her."

Wyatt rolled his eyes. "You're a religious nut, aren't you. All this piety and purity, it's so quaint."

Tears streamed from Lydia's eyes. She couldn't believe what she was hearing.

"Why do you even want to marry her if this is how you want to live?"

"Never said I was gonna marry her?"

Lydia gasped again and her tears increased.

"Why not?"

Wyatt shrugged. "I'm getting tired of her. My father made us get engaged, said he owed it to his friend, her father. At first I didn't mind going along with it, but I wasn't counting on her being so religious."

"How can you treat her like that? Why not let her go if you don't want to marry her?"

"It comes down to money." Wyatt flashed him a smarmy smile.

"Money?" It was all Jake could do to not drive his fist into the man's throat.

"Yeah, she doesn't know thi,s but her father left some money for her and her brother. Pa will give it to her when she's twenty-one. Figured I'd marry her then, and the money would be mine and I could put her away or find some way to dispose of her... I'm not gonna marry her until then, I'll put up with her for a time, until I get the money. That's about all I can stand. I figure I only have to look at those weird eyes and red hair for two more years then I'll be a wealthy man."

Jake could keep his temper no longer. He pulled his hand back and punched Wyatt in the face, and the man's head flew back against the rails of the corral. Wyatt groaned and leaped up on Jake's back, forcing him to the ground. The two men wrestled and fought, both taking and giving blows. Jake pinned Wyatt to the ground, thrusting one arm across his neck, with the other he punched the man again. Myrtle sat against the back wall of the stall and begged them to stop.

Eli stopped walking and a foreboding feeling came over him. "Sylv." She stood up and ran to him. "I have to go to Jake. I can't explain but I have to."

She nodded and kissed him and he turned and sprinted toward the livery. He arrived in time to see Lydia sob and run away. He heard the yelling and the voice of a woman begging both men to stop. Eli walked in and dragged Jake off Wyatt. "Jake, this isn't the way."

Jake pulled against him, blood ran down his face and a cut above his eye was beginning to bruise. "Let me go." He scowled to Wyatt who was rubbing his jaw.

Wyatt lunged at Jake and poked his chest. "You're gonna be sorry, Jenkins."

"You don't deserve her," Jake spat.

"Enough!" Eli yelled. "Go sober up, Wyatt." He scowled and eyed the woman who was still holding her blouse closed. It was obvious to him what Jake was upset about. He gripped his friend's shoulder. "Come on, Jake. You need to calm down."

He nodded and allowed Eli to escort him out.

Eli marched his friend around the corner and finally released his arm. "What was that about?"

Jake sniffed loudly. His face was in agony but he didn't care. He didn't care about the pain in his ribs either. He couldn't remember a time when he'd ever been so angry.

"What do you think?" He sneered at Eli.

Eli raised his brows. "I think it's not me you're angry at."

Jake exhaled loudly. "Sorry. That man made me wild. He's in there cheating on her and it's not the first time. He admitted as much. Told me he's only with Lydia because she stands to inherit money when she turns twenty-one. He plans to string her along and marry her just before her birthday, claim her money and put her off somehow. He's scum. You should've let me finish him."

Eli nodded. "Can't do that. It'd be you that would get in trouble with the law, then you'd be no good to Miss Howard. She's gonna need support, after hearing that."

"What do you mean?"

"I saw her run away from the livery. I imagine she overheard everything."

Jake's face curled up in pain. "Ohhh, how awful for her. He said some cruel things about her. Told me she was ugly and all. I need to find her, where did she run to?"

"I don't know. But I think you should wait." Eli raised his brows and clutched his friend's shoulder.

"I can't, she needs me."

"Does she?"

Jake exhaled. "I can't bear to see her hurt. I have to go to her."

"Jake, you need to take this slowly. I know you love her but she'll be very fragile."

"Thank you, Cupid. I know what I'm doing."

"I know, Friend, I just know how angry and hurt you are right now."

Jake took a deep breath. "I know. I just want to comfort her."

Eli nodded. "I'll pray for you both. And don't worry, I'll deal with Wyatt. I'll suggest he leave town and never come back."

"Which way did she go?"

Eli gestured toward town. Jake nodded to his friend and hurried away.

He searched for close to an hour and couldn't find Lydia anywhere. He paused and prayed for divine inspiration and an idea sprang to his mind. He made his way toward the small lake at the back of town There was a pretty little bay there that was a favourite with many in the town. He reached the bay and found Lydia face down in the long grass by the river's edge, sobbing.

"Ohhhh." He ran over and threw himself down next to her and touched her back. "Miss Howard?"

She sobbed loudly and sat up and threw herself against his chest. He gulped and wrapped his arms around her. He lay his head on hers and rocked gently back and forth, whispering soothing words to her. Her pain made his heart ache. Holding her was such a privilege, even though he hated to see her cry. He imagined what it would be like to hold her for the rest of his days. It was some time before she calmed and even more time before she sat up again. When at last she raised her sad, mismatched eyes at him, her lip trembled.

Jake pulled a clean handkerchief from his top pocket and offered it to her. She gave him a sad smile and wiped at her eyes. "I'm sorry," she whispered and hung her head.

Jake reached a hand up to lift her chin. "Why are you sorry?" Compassion and sorrow filled his dark eyes.

"I'm here sobbing like a child."

"I don't blame you. Eli told me you overheard what Wyatt said."

"I can't believe he'd do that to me. I knew he wasn't exactly the romantic type, but how can he be so cruel?"

Jake's heart was breaking. He didn't know how to help this lovely girl. All he knew was that he desperately wanted to take away her pain. "I don't know. All I know for sure is he doesn't deserve you."

She looked shyly up at him. "I'm not so sure about that. Maybe the problem is me."

"What?" Jake's brow curled up. "Why would you say that?"

She raised and lowered her shoulders. "I'm funny looking. I know I am. Red hair, freckles and two different-colored eyes. That's why I was obliged to stay with him. It's the only way I can have a home. He told me more than once I wouldn't get a man on my own looking like I do"

"Why?"

"No one will want to marry an ugly woman like me. I've been picked on my whole life because of my eyes." She hung her head again.

Jake lifted her chin, looked into her eyes and gave her a wide smile. "I can't stop looking at your eyes."

"Because they're so weird?" She frowned.

He stroked her cheek. "No, because they're so amazing. The green one has these mesmerizing flecks of golden-brown and one is as clear and blue as the sky over my ranch. I can't get enough of them. I've never met a woman who looks like you."

"You're probably better off."

Jake squeezed her arm gently and explored her face with his eyes. "Don't say that. You're a beautiful woman, Miss Howard."

Lydia lowered her head and sighed. "You're just saying that to make me feel better."

Jake cupped her cheek. "No, I really am not. I've thought you were beautiful from the moment I met you. When I carried you to the clinic that day I knocked you down, I noticed how beautiful you were and I've not been able to get you out of my mind since."

"Really?"

"Really."

"Why didn't you say something?"

He smirked. "You weren't free; I'd never proposition someone else's girl." He sighed. "No matter how I feel," he muttered under his breath.

Lydia blushed. "And now?"

On the tip of his tongue were promises and love but he heard Eli's words ringing in his mind. He smiled and stroked her cheek. "And now I'd like a chance to get to know you, more. You're so unique and lovely."

She smiled. "I'd like that too, Mr. Jenkins. You've always been so kind to me."

"Please, call me Jake?"

"Only if you'll call me Lydia."

He smiled. "That's a pretty name, one of my favorite names."

Lydia's face lit up. "Really?"

"Really."

She smiled. Jake grinned at her. "What?" She lifted her eyes to him.

"I love your smile. The way your face lights up and those amazing eyes. You're so beautiful."

"Thank you, Jake." She lowered her eyes and her cheeks grew red.

He nodded. "Come on, I'll help you back to town."

"What am I supposed to do now?" Her lip quivered and her eyes displayed her fear.

"What do you mean?"

"I can't go back to Wyatt now."

"Of course you can't, he doesn't deserve you. Eli said he'd drive Wyatt out of town. I imagine he's gone already."

Tears flooded Lydia's eyes.

"What is it?"

"What am I supposed to do now?"

Jake frowned.

"My teacher's salary won't cover the boarding house and my expenses. It was all just temporary till the wedding."

"Don't worry about any of that."

"But I have to. I'm reliant on him to survive. I don't have but pennies to my name. All of my salary went straight to him and he paid for everything. I suppose I can sell my engagement ring but it's not real and not worth very much. I have nowhere to go." Her tears came again.

Jake touched her arm and brushed a tear off her cheek. "Please, don't worry about that. I'll make sure you're taken care of."

"I can't ask you to do that."

"You didn't ask me. I offered."

"But why would you do that?"

He gave her a broad grin and fixed his eyes on hers. "Because I care about you." It wasn't what he wanted to say, but Eli was right; he needed to take this slowly.

"Thank you. I don't know how to repay you." She hung her head.

"You don't need to. I want to do this for you. After all, it's my fault things have gone pear-shaped with Wyatt."

"In some ways, I'm glad they have. I wasn't in love with him; I just didn't really have much choice." She shrugged.

"I know. It broke my heart to see you with him. I wish you hadn't been."

"I had no choice. I'm an orphan. I have no money. I was just doing what I thought I had to do to survive." She looked up at him. Tears flooded the corners of her mismatched eyes again, and Jake gently wiped an escapee off her cheek.

"I will make sure you're looked after. You have my word on that."

Lydia blushed. "You're very kind, Jake."

He dared to tuck a tress of hair behind her ear. "You deserve to be treated kindly."

"Jake." Lydia's cheeks reddened more. "I don't know what to say."

"You don't have to say anything. I like you very much. I think you know that. I'd love to get to know you, Lydia Howard. But I know your heart is very fragile right now and I want nothing more than your happiness. I won't ask more of you than your friendship, at least for now."

She took a deep breath and smiled shyly. "Thank you. I'd like that. I'm afraid it might take me some time to be ready for anything else."

Jake brushed her cheek with his knuckles and smiled. "You take all the time you need. I'm not going anywhere."

"Thank you."

He nodded. "Come on, let's go back to town." Jake stood up and put his hand down to Lydia. She took it and allowed him to help her up. She leaned her head against his chest and he wrapped his arms around her again.

She sighed loudly.

"What is it?" Jake murmured against her hair.

"I've never been held in someone's arms like this before."

"Really?"

"Really, not since my father died."

Jake tightened his arms and squeezed her gently. "Well anytime you want to be held, I'm here." He lay his cheek against her hair.

"Thank you," she whispered.

He kissed her hair. "It's my pleasure." He stopped himself before he called her 'darling.' It was all he could do to resist kissing her, but it wasn't the time. She needed time to recover; that was only fair. He'd never dream of rushing her. He cared far too much for her to do anything to hurt her. For now it was enough she was out of the control of that horrible man.

She stepped back from Jake and smiled. "Thank you for your kindness, and for sticking up for me. I'm sorry for how horrible Wyatt was to you." She put a hand to his bruised eye. "I'm sorry he hurt you."

"I don't care about that. I'm just glad you're free of him. He wasn't good enough for you. You deserve to be treated special. I'd take a thousand blows to make that happen."

"Thank you, Jake."

Jake winked at her and offered her his arm. She smiled and took it, allowing him to lead her back to town.

Ten

Eli exited the livery as Jake and Lydia reached town. He paused and watched them, raised his brows and thrust his arms over his chest. A wry smile crossed his face. He couldn't help but think they looked good together.

Jake approached and released her arm. "Eli." He couldn't keep the sparkle from his eyes and Eli knew something had changed.

"I'm so sorry, Miss Howard. I heard what happened."

"Thank you, Mr. Jackson. I appreciate that."

"I want you to know Wyatt has left town. He won't be back. If he does come back, he'll have more than just Jake to contend with." Eli gritted his teeth for a moment. He couldn't abide cruelty to any person, especially the innocent.

Jake nodded his thanks to his friend.

Eli returned his nod and then gently touched Lydia's arm. "Are you okay now?"

"Yes thank you. Jake has been most kind to me."

Eli nodded knowingly. "Well if there's anything you need, let me know."

"Thank you. I best get back to the picnic."

"Do you want me to come with you?" Jake offered.

Lydia put a hand on his arm and smiled at him. "No, thank you, Jake. I'll be just fine." She stood up on her toes and kissed him on the cheek. "Thank you."

Without a further word she turned and hurried back to the common.

Jake grinned and lifted his hand to his cheek as he watched her walk away.

Eli pursed his lips and raised his brows at his friend. "What?"

"You look a little happier than last time I spoke to you."

"Of course I'm happy, she's away from that monster."

"And?"

Jake frowned. "And what?"

"Are you courting?"

"No, you were right; it's much too soon for that. She'll need time to heal. She's worried about how she'll survive. She was completely reliant on that man and didn't think she could do, or deserved, any better." Jake grimaced.

Eli chuckled. "Well, that kiss'll keep you goin' in the meantime."

Jake's face lit up. "It sure will. And she threw herself in my arms while she cried. There's nothing like holding her and being there for her and not having to worry about that man."

Eli gripped his friend's shoulder. "I wish you both every happiness."

"Thank you. I know it'll be some time before she's ready to court, if ever, but even if she's never ready I'm just glad she's free of him."

Eli and Jake wandered slowly back toward the common. Jake had his hands in his pockets and a contented gleam in his eyes. *I get the feeling my future is about to change for good.* He still hadn't completely let go of Chrissy yet, but she was rapidly being replaced by Lydia and now that Lydia wasn't a forbidden love, he was free to let himself love her. He'd wait a lifetime for her to be ready.

Eli nodded to his friend and returned to join his fiancée.

Jake kept walking and resumed his seat, leaning against the tree with his family.

Jarrod, Vi and Mrs. Jenkins looked at each other then at Jake's bruised face.

Jarrod raised his brows and cleared his throat. Jake looked up and a slow smile crossed his face. "What?"

Three faces looked at him.

"What?" he asked again.

"You left here with a face of thunder and return looking like the cat who got the mouse, with bruises on your chin." Jarrod crossed his arms and pursed his lips.

Jake shrugged. "Miss Howard is no longer betrothed to Wyatt McCain."

Jarrod grinned, and the three looked at each other again.

"So you're free to court her then?" Elsie asked, her heart singing with joy.

"In time. She'll not be ready for a while, I imagine. She's pretty fragile after all that. I've agreed to help pay her way. She was completely reliant on him."

"Doesn't she have a salary?" Vi stroked her abdomen as she spoke.

"Yes but she gave every cent to Wyatt and it isn't very much. She's had no choice but to rely on Wyatt all this time." Jake's eyes sparkled. "But I'll make sure she's taken care of." He grinned and added, "for the rest of her days if it's up to me."

Jarrod nodded and smiled at his brother.

"Oh, Son. I'm so glad for you." Elsie gripped his arm. "She's a lovely girl."

"I think so." Jake touched the cheek where she'd kissed him and his face reddened.

Jarrod slapped his back, beyond relieved his brother wasn't hurting anymore.

*　*　*　*

Jake woke the next morning before the rooster had even lifted his head from his slumber. He rose and spent time with the Lord, then mounted his horse and galloped into town. He dismounted at the school house and hurried up the stairs, lit the fire in the stove and hauled an armload of wood from the shed behind the classroom. He noticed a patch of orange flowers growing near the small shed and grinned. Hurrying back out, he gathered a handful and slipped them into a jar he found on a shelf.

It was a small gesture but he hoped it would make Lydia smile. He hoped to make her smile for the rest of his days.

He hurried out again and walked to the livery to stow his horse. He was surprised to find Eli inside. "You're up early?"

Eli put down his pitchfork. "I could say the same for you." He raised his brows in question.

"I wanted to light the stove in the schoolroom. It's not really cold yet, but I wanted to save Lydia a job."

Eli grinned and shook his head. "Now who's got it bad?"

"I'm not sure about that. It's just nice to have someone to care about again. It's thrilling." Jake's eyes sparkled.

"I'm glad. But heed my warning, don't be in a hurry."

"I'm not. She needs time and I understand. I plan to be there for her in the meantime. I need to make sure she's taken care of. I'm headed to the bank to make arrangements to cover her board."

Eli nodded. "I hope you aren't setting yourself up for more hurt."

"I've got my eyes open, Eli. Even if she never wants to court. I'm just glad she's free of him. I'd give everything I own for that."

Eli nodded. "You're a good man, Jake Jenkins. I truly hope this works out for you."

"Thank you." Jake nodded. "So, ready to be a groom in two weeks?"

"Beyond ready."

"Where're you gonna live? Surely not in your little cabin at the back." Jake grimaced.

"Of course not. What do you take me for?"

"Well, where are you gonna live?"

"I've purchased the old Miller house."

Jake nodded knowingly. "That's a nice little house, it would've set you back some."

"It was reasonable. They wanted to sell up and I got it for a steal. Sylvia's over the moon, especially since it's so close to her father's home."

"Is she working?"

"Part time in the dress store."

"Will she keep working once you're married?"

"I hope so. Not that we need it. Heck, business is growing, and I have my grandfather's small bequest. I'm fortunate compared to most, but she enjoys working."

Jake merely nodded. "Well I best get going. There's a lovely school teacher who needs an escort to school." He grinned.

"She needs an escort, does she?"

"Yep."

Eli reached for Duke's rein and walked the horse into a stall, chuckling at the wry grin on his friend's face.

* * * *

Jake waited in the foyer of the boarding house. He'd been to the bank as soon as it opened and paid four months in advance. That would take her through to Christmas. Beyond that, he'd see what happened.

"Good Mornin,' Mr. Jenkins."

Jake smiled at Mrs. Tina Evans the boarding house proprietor. "Good morning, Ma'am. I hope you don't mind me waiting here."

"Who ya waitin' for?"

"Miss Howard." He couldn't help but grin.

The older woman raised her brows. "Very good. You can wait in the foyer, would you care for a cup of coffee?"

"Thank you, Ma'am."

She nodded and hurried away. Jake wandered out to the foyer. Mrs. Evans brought him a cup and he nodded his thanks. He leaned back against the wall and waited. He looked around, it was a large house, but somewhat rundown and dingy. He hated that she had to live here; surely he could find something better for her. *To think Wyatt lived in that cabin and made her live here!* She deserved better than this. He drained his cup and stroked his chin as he tried to think of other options. He was deep in thought and didn't hear Lydia approach.

She stopped in her tracks when she saw him and grinned. "Jake Jenkins what are you doing here?"

He snapped out of his reverie and stepped forward. She was dressed so simply, but looked absolutely lovely to him. He explored her face and got lost in those amazing eyes.

Lydia blushed.

At last Jake found his voice. "I wanted to walk you to school."

"Thank you."

Wordlessly he reached for her books and basket. She smiled her thanks and slid her arm under his extended elbow. He grinned at Mrs. Evans as he escorted Lydia out the door.

Jake's heart pounded and his chest expanded. He was sure his buttons would pop at any moment. It was such a delight to have her on his arm. They walked slowly and he led her up the stairs and pushed open the schoolhouse doors. She frowned. "The stove is on?"

"I know." Jake winked at her.

"Why did you do that?"

"I wanted to spare you the job."

"Jake, I can light the stove."

"Of course you can and I won't be able to do it every day, but I wanted to spare you the job this once."

"Thank you. You're very kind."

"It's my pleasure."

He led her to the desk and placed her basket and books down. She let go his arm and gasped. "And are you responsible for the flowers too?"

"Yes, Ma'am. Flowers for the teacher." He winked.

"Jake. You don't have to do all these things for me."

"I know I don't have to."

"Thank you. But I don't expect you to."

"Just enjoy it, Lydia. I want to serve you when I can."

"I'm not used to this." She shrugged.

"Well get used to it." He grinned and looked into her eyes. He tucked a curl behind her ear. "I want to show you how you deserve to be treated." He paused and smiled. "And treasured."

"Jake." Lydia's eyes sparkled.

He smiled. "Your eyes are so beautiful."

"You don't think it's weird that I have two different-colored eyes?"

"Not at all. May I ask a question?"

"Sure." She smiled.

"Do you know why they're like that?"

She shrugged. "I don't know why, but it's hereditary. My mother and grandmother had it too, apparently. It seems to be passed down to the women in the family."

Jake smiled. "And I hope one day you have a little red-haired girl with the same eyes."

Lydia blushed. "Oh, Jake." She lowered her head and a dark pink rose on her cheeks. His gentle manner was so foreign to her. Wyatt had never showed her any affection unless it suited him, and she never got the feeling he was trying to care for her. But whenever Jake was around, she felt like the most special person in the world. It was overwhelming.

She looked up at the clock. "Oh, I better get ready for the day."

"First, I was wondering. Would you let me pray with you?"

Lydia closed her eyes and sighed. When she opened them they glistened with tears.

"What is it?" He brushed away an escapee from her cheek.

"It's what I dreamed off, being able to share my faith with the man I..." She caught herself and blushed deeply. "That is, a man I'm getting to know."

He grinned. "We'll share devotions, too when you're ready, but for now, I want to pray with you."

She nodded. He took both her hands in his and spoke a quick prayer over her and the students that would sit in those seats. Lydia echoed his 'Amen' and raised damp eyes to his. She lifted a hand to his chest. "Thank you," she whispered.

"You're welcome, Miss Howard." He winked at her and brushed her cheek. "Have a good day."

"Thank you."

"You're welcome. I'll be rather busy this week I'm sorry to say, but will you let me take you to supper on Friday evening?"

"Of course, Jake. I'd like that."

He leaned in and kissed her cheek, then looked into her eyes. "See you, Friday." He winked again and turned on his heels to leave, with his heart singing in his chest.

Lydia stood for a moment and put her hand to her cheek. His gentle kiss still lingered there. She closed her eyes and sighed. "Oh, Lord, please bless Jake." She smiled, took a deep breath, and walked out to ring the bell.

Eleven

Jake pulled the chair out for Lydia and seated her, then took the seat opposite her at the café.

"Thank you for this, Jake. It's kind of you."

"You don't have to keep thanking me. It's the least I can do."

Lydia grinned. "It's so new to me. I'm not used to being treated so kindly."

"I told you, get used to it." He winked and caught Hannah-Mae's eye. She pulled the pencil and notebook from her apron pocket and hurried over to them.

Jake didn't need to look at the menu. He grinned at Hannah-Mae. "The usual please."

The waitress smiled and nodded. "Meatloaf and mashed potatoes."

Jake grinned his thanks and they both turned to look at Lydia to wait for her to order.

"Ummmm." She grimaced and perused the menu. "I'll just have a baked potato." She pointed to the list.

Hannah-Mae nodded and scribbled it down.

"Is that all you want?" Jake frowned.

Lydia shrugged and her cheeks reddened. She lowered her eyes and spoke in a quiet voice. "It's all I can afford."

Jake furrowed his brow. "Lydia, get what you want. I'll cover it."

"I can't ask you to do that; you've already done so much for me."

Jake raised his brows. "I want to, Lydia. Please let me." He gripped her hand.

"Very well. I'll have chicken fried steak with the baked potato."

"Would you like vegetables with that?" Hannah-Mae paused with her pencil hovering over the page.

Lydia's cheeks colored. It seemed so lush and expensive. Wyatt would never let her have anything extra than the bare minimum, if he took her out to eat at all. And he certainly wouldn't waste his money on dessert for her.

"Yes, she would. And we'll both have coffee and we'll have ice cream and chocolate cake for dessert please," Jake offered. Hannah-Mae added to their order and hurried away. Jake looked at Lydia. She hung her head.

"What is it? I'm sorry for ordering for you. If you don't like what I ordered you can change it. I just didn't want you to feel bad about the money."

She lifted shining eyes to him. "But, Jake, I do feel bad."

"Why?"

"You shouldn't have to pay for everything for me."

"Why not? You're worth it and I can afford it."

"But I feel like I have no way of repaying you and your kindness to me."

He reached for one of her hands and held it in both of his. "Lydia, I care for you deeply. I want us to court."

She gasped and bit her lip.

"I know you aren't ready and that's fine. I'll wait as long as you need me to. In the meantime, I'll be here for you, in whatever capacity you need me. A friend, a confidant, whatever you need. I want to take care of you. I hope that one day you'll take care of me too." He blushed and so did she. "But for now, taking care of you and your fragile heart, is a pleasure for me." He reached across and stroked her cheek. "Please don't feel bad and don't worry about needing to pay me back. That doesn't matter to me, I'm not keeping score; I only do that with my brother."

She managed a shaky smile and sniffed away the threatening tears. Wyatt kept track of every cent she'd cost him and reminded her of it often. Jake brushed away a tear that streaked down her cheek. His eyes asked the question.

"I'm sorry. It's just so new to me. And I'm sorry for making you wait..."

He lifted his hand to stop her. "No, don't be sorry. It's far more important to me that your heart heals, thoroughly. Trust me, I know it is not an overnight process. It's my pleasure to help you through it."

"I'm so glad God brought me here. Even with all that happened with Wyatt, because it got me here. I'm happier now than I've been in many years, thanks to you."

"I'm so glad." He stroked the soft hand. "And I want you to know, even if you're never ready, I'm still glad you're free of him. I just want you to be happy."

She smiled and they were interrupted by Hannah-Mae bringing their food.

They enjoyed their meal, and dessert and lingered over their coffee and conversation. Afterward, Jake escorted her back to the boarding house. He entered the wide foyer and frowned. "I wish you didn't have to live here."

"What's wrong with the boarding house?"

"You deserve better."

"Oh, Jake, this is fine. I get my meals provided and my room is ample." She shrugged and continued, "I don't own very much, so I don't need much space. One day I'd like to have a home of my own, but for now I'm content here. I've made some good friends in the boarding house."

"Well in that case I'm glad." He fixed his dark eyes on hers. "And I'm certain one day you'll have that home of your own." *You will if I have anything to do with it.*

"Well I'd better turn in."

"First, if it's not too forward, would you go to the dance with me?"

"Which dance?"

"The church social."

"That's not till the end of October."

"I know, just getting in early before you get snapped up by someone else."

She laughed. "Of course, Jake, I'd like that."

"And one more thing."

She tilted her head to the side in anticipation.

He took a deep breath. "My best friend, Eli, is getting married on Saturday. Would you come? I'll be his best man but I'll sit with you at the supper, and I hope you'll honor me with a dance."

Lydia shrugged.

He raised his brows. "Please, I'll be the perfect gentlemen. I'm not trying to rush you. Don't consider it courtin'. I'd just like to spend time with you, and I want to get to know you, Lydia."

Lydia grinned. "In that case, I'd like to." She stood up on her toes and kissed his cheek. "See you at the service."

"See you at the service," he murmured and watched her walk away. He took a deep breath and raised his hand to his cheek. Mrs. Evans walked out of the kitchen and saw the end of the scene. She noticed the gleam in his eyes and chuckled as she hurried to her bedroom.

* * * *

Jake stopped the wagon outside the church and helped his mother down. He led her to their row, seated her, and then hurried out the door. He walked down the stairs and across the road toward the boarding house. Lydia walked up the boardwalk with her Bible under her arm. She wore a pale green gown with a matching hat. Jake felt his heart flip-flop in his chest. She looked so much more mature than her nineteen years.

"Good morning, Ma'am." He grinned and put his arm out to her, reaching for her Bible with his other hand. She smiled and passed it over gladly, taking his arm. He turned and walked her to the church.

"Jake, you didn't have to come and get me. I've been walking to church on my own since I came here, it's only a hundred yards away." She gestured across the road to the church.

"Lydia, I'm well aware of how strong and independent you are, and I admire that. But there's nothing wrong with relying on someone from time to time."

She smiled and squeezed his arm. "Thank you, I've never had someone I could rely on before."

"It's my pleasure. I'll do my utmost to make sure you can always rely on me." He grinned. He'd never tire of having her on his arm. He led her to the church and seated her next to his mother. "Ma, you remember Miss Howard?" He grinned as he sat on the end of the row.

"Yes, lovely to see you, Miss Howard."

"Thank you, Mrs. Jenkins. You as well."

"That's a pretty dress."

"Thank you. It's my only Sunday dress."

"Well it's lovely."

Lydia smiled kindly. Jake grinned. He leaned back in the pew and took a deep breath. Her proximity was thrilling. Being able to sit with her in church and share this with her was wonderful. Chrissy had always sat with her family, at least up until they got engaged. He fought to keep his mind focused as the smell of Lydia's perfume wafted into his nostrils. It made his head spin. He took another deep breath and forced his feelings into line. He nodded to Eli and Sylvia as they walked in arm in arm and entered the row in front of them.

Eli gave his friend a knowing smile and seated Sylvia before taking his seat next to her.

The pastor raised his hands to get their attention and the service began.

Jake was acutely aware of the woman next to him. He couldn't help but let his mind wander to what it would be like to have her in his row permanently and in his heart. He stood for the prayer and tried to remember Chrissy's face. He furrowed his brows. He struggled to recall her, and inhaled sharply as he realised the thought of her no longer bought pain. Was he free of her? No! Not completely. But she was rapidly being replaced with Lydia in his heart. He dragged his thoughts back to the present and lifted the hymn book so that Lydia could see it too. He grinned as he heard her sweet voice lifted in praise next to him. He raised his own voice and accompanied her.

He waited for Lydia to sit, then sat next to her and poked the hymnbook into the wooden slot on the back of the pew before him and sat back to enjoy the service.

At last the pastor prayed the final benediction. Jake opened his eyes in surprise as he felt her soft hand slip into his large one. He squeezed the hand and smiled, thanking the Lord. She was beginning to give him her heart.

Twelve

"Would you care to dance?" Jake put a hand out to Lydia.

"I'd like that." She smiled and allowed herself to be led.

Jake took her in his arms and they fell into the rhythm of the waltz. Lydia looked up at him. "What's got you grinning like that?"

"Isn't it obvious?"

She shook her head and furrowed her brows.

He fixed his eyes on hers. "I'm here at my best friend's wedding dancing with a beautiful woman in my arms. It couldn't get any better!"

"Oh, Jake." Lydia blushed.

"I mean it. You're beautiful. That dress is lovely and you make it even lovelier." He stroked her cheek.

"You look pretty good yourself. That's a nice suit."

Jake laughed. "It's the only one I own. Not much use for a three-piece suit on the ranch."

Lydia chuckled. "I can imagine. But I'm certain we can find more reasons for you to wear it the future."

Jake nodded and squinted at her. "We?"

Lydia's cheeks reddened and she tucked her lips under and raised her brows.

Jake stroked her cheek. "Miss Howard? Explain yourself." He was oblivious to all the couples dancing around him. "What do you mean by we?"

Lydia fixed eyes on him and gave him a shy smile. "What do you think it means?" She tucked her lips under.

Jake's heart soared. He took her hand and led her out onto the boardwalk. He put his hands on her waist and looked into her eyes. "Are you saying you're ready?"

She nodded and her cheeks reddened. "But I want you to ask me."

Jake's smile grew wide. "With pleasure! Lydia Howard. Will you let me call on you?"

"Of course, Jake."

"Yahoo! I couldn't dream you'd be ready so soon."

"My heart is still fragile, but you make me so safe and loved that I can't help it."

He cupped her cheek and fixed his eyes on hers. His gaze became intense. "You'll always be safe and loved with me. I promise."

She merely nodded.

"You're so beautiful. Your eyes are glowing."

"My weird eyes." She lowered her head.

Jake frowned, and lifted her chin. "Stop that. They aren't weird, they're unique and beautiful and I love them. I love that you have two different-colored eyes. Truly, it's captivating." His voice grew to a whisper as a shy smile crossed her face. Her full pink lips were tantalizing. He lowered his head and they shared a sweet, soft kiss. He pulled back from her; her eyes remained closed and her lips trembled.

She opened her eyes and a dreamy look crossed her face. "Oh, Jake."

He stroked her cheek. "You're so lovely."

"Oh, Jake." It was all she could think to say. She lay her head against his chest and he put his arms around her and lay his head against hers.

"I love you," he murmured into her hair.

"Oh, Jake," she said a third time then pulled back and looked up at him. "I love you too."

Jake closed his eyes and leaned his head back. He looked back at her and grinned. "Those are the sweetest words I could ever hear. It's such a joy to have you love me."

"You too, Jake. I never knew what love could feel like. But being here in your arms, it's the most wonderful feeling." She grinned and lifted a soft hand to his cheek. "I never felt this way about Wyatt. He never once held me or kissed me."

"I'm sorry you went through that."

"I'm not. I'm glad I never had any of that with Wyatt, because now you'll be the first and only man I ever kiss, the first and only man who's arms have held me and it's wonderful." She blushed. "Sorry for getting ahead of myself."

"Don't be. I'll always be here to hold you, Darling. I promise."

An icy wind blew past and she shivered.

"Ohhh, come on let's go back inside. You'll catch your death of cold. Nothing like the cold of a prairie wind this time of year."

She stopped him before he removed his arms from hers and stood up on her toes and kissed him again. She stepped back and blushed. "I'm sorry if that was too forward."

He grinned and winked at her. "Not at all. I liked it very much. Any time you want to kiss me, my lips'll be happy to oblige."

They both chuckled. He put his hand out and she took it and they walked back inside hand in hand.

Jake and Lydia approached the newlyweds. Eli had his arm around his new wife and he kissed her temple. He raised his brows at Jake and gestured to their joined hands. "What does this mean?"

"Not to steal your day, but..." Jake raised the hand he held to his lips. "...We're courting."

Lydia blushed.

Eli grinned and slapped his friend on the back. "I'm not worried about you stealing our day at all. I'm thrilled for you both."

Lydia smiled.

Eli let go of his wife and embraced Lydia. "I'm pleased for you. He's a good man," he whispered into her hair.

"Thank you."

Lydia embraced Sylvia and they congratulated each other.

"Well we need to get to our honeymoon." Eli grinned and Sylvia blushed.

"First you have to throw your bouquet." Lydia smiled.

"You're right." Sylvia smiled as all the single girls lined up. She threw it over her head and whirled around to see a blushing Lydia with the bouquet in her hands.

Jake's face lit up and Eli slapped his back. "I said you'd be next."

"I hope so."

"Good for you. Now I must take my bride on our honeymoon."

"Of course. Congratulations, my friend." Jake embraced Eli.

*   *   *   *

"So how was the honeymoon?"

Eli looked up at Jake and grinned. "Wonderful, I'm thrilled to have that woman loving me."

"I know what you mean."

Eli nodded. "I can see the sparkle in your eyes."

"I'm not surprised. I've been courting Lydia a week and It's been the best week of my life."

"Better than with Chrissy?"

Jake screwed up his face. "Not better so much as different. They're very different women."

"So are you over Chrissy now?"

Jake paused for a time, screwed up his face and rubbed his chin. "I'm not sure I ever will be. I loved her, I was going to marry her. I think a part of her will always be in my heart in a way."

"I understand, but the love you have for Lydia is different, so it occupies a different space, or at least in a different way."

"Yeah that's it exactly. Like Chrissy is a lovely memory of the past, but Lydia is my present and I sure hope she's my future."

Eli raised his brows. "You making plans?"

"I think I am. I know it's only been a short time…"

Eli cut him off. "I understand, I knew I wanted to marry Sylvia from the start, and I imagine after all you and Lydia have faced, now that you've found each other you'll never want to let each other go."

"That's it exactly."

"What does your family think of her?"

"Ma adores Lydia and they have a lot in common. Ma was orphaned at a young age, so neither really knew their mother. Ma's become like a mother to Lydia even in a short time. And Jarrod's got his head in the clouds so he's barely noticed."

"He's going to be a father soon. I can't blame him."

"Yes." Jake grinned.

"Well I'm pleased for you, Jake. Now that you know, don't wait too long. You deserve to be happy with a family of your own."

Jake nodded. "I'm planning to look at rings tonight."

"Good for you."

"Thank you. I hope I can be as happy as you and have that same goofy look on my face that you have."

Eli laughed outright. "You already do, Friend, it's good to see."

Both men laughed together and Jake left his horse with his friend, and hurried out to walk the lovely teacher to school.

Thirteen

"Thank you for taking me to the dance. I had the most enchanting night." Lydia grinned as they strolled toward the boarding house in the moonlight.

"It's my pleasure. You know I felt like I was dancing with Cinderella."

"Oh, Jake, you're the kindest man I've ever known."

Jake stopped walking and pulled her into his arms. "And you're the loveliest woman I know." He looked into her eyes and they gazed at each other in silence for a time.

Jake could bear it no more. He pushed her from him and put his hand in his pocket. He knelt down in the middle of the street and took her hand.

"Jake, what are you...?" She gasped.

"Lydia, I know this may seem sudden, but I'm in love with you and I don't ever want to be without you."

Lydia placed her spare hand on his cheek. "Oh, Jake, I love you, too."

He grinned. "Will you marry me?"

Lydia's eyes filled with tears and she put her hand to her mouth.

Jake frowned, not knowing what her reaction meant. Lydia grinned at him and his face lit up.

"Yes, Jake, of course I'll marry you."

He grinned, leaped up in the air and punched the sky. "Yahooo." He scooped her up into his arms and she flung hers around his neck.

"I love you so much, Lydia Howard. I can't wait to marry you."

"I love you too, Jake." She leaned in and kissed him, and they both eagerly prolonged the kiss.

Jake didn't put her down. He stood looking into her mesmerising mismatched eyes. "You're rather extraordinary."

"Thank you. I don't deserve you, Jake."

Jake put her down and put a hand on her cheek. "Yes you do. You deserve the whole world. I love you so much."

"Jake?"

"Yeah?"

"May I have the ring?"

Jake chuckled. "Of course."

He flicked open the box and held it out to her.

"Oh, it's lovely."

Jake lifted it out and slipped it on her finger. A green stone sat between clear glass stones. "I'm glad you like it."

"Thank you, I love it."

"You don't need to thank me. Now come on, I'll walk you to your room."

She nodded and took his offered hand.

"I'll have to work on finding a house in town for us to live in."

"You don't want us to live on the ranch?"

"Don't you want to be close to school?"

"Why?"

"You're the teacher, remember?"

"Jake, I won't teach once we're married."

He paused and turned to look at her. "You won't? How come?"

"Don't you want me to be at home, to be a wife?"

"Yes of course, but I want you to be happy and I know how much you love teaching."

"Do you want me teach when we're married?"

"Yes, if you want to. I'd never ask you to give it up for me. I'll miss you every moment you're gone, but you're a gifted teacher and the children need you. So I want you to make the choice that is right for you, my love."

Lydia's face lit up and she threw herself in his arms. "Thank you, Jake. I've never had someone put me first before."

He pulled back from her and cupped her soft cheek. "Get used to it. You'll always be my first priority. Apart from the Lord, I'll live to serve you all my days."

"Oh, Jake." She kissed him and they continued walking. "I want us to live on the ranch. It's your home and I want to be there with you. I'll finish out the semester and then I want to concentrate on being your wife."

Jake paused again to look her in the eye, and a tear streaked down his cheek. "Are you absolutely sure that's what you want?" He sniffed.

"Yes, of course. Why the tears?"

"I can't believe you're willing to do that for me."

"You were willing to move to town for me. It's what you do when you love someone."

"Thank you. I appreciate it more than you know. I'm the most blessed man on earth and you are going to be the most wonderful wife.."

"You're welcome. I can't wait to make a home for you, and our family." She blushed.

"I'm starting to regret giving my cabin to my brother."

"Why?"

"I guess I'll have to build us another one on the ranch."

"Why?"

"Don't you want to have a home of your own?"

"What's wrong with the house you live in now?"

"You want to live there?"

"Yes, of course, it's a lovely home."

"We'll have to build a cottage for Ma."

"No, please, she must stay with us."

"But don't you want the house to yourself?"

"It's big enough that we'll have our own space. I never had a mother and I've come to treasure yours so much. Please, let her stay with us as long as she wants to." A tear escaped Jake's eye and Lydia reached up to brush it off. "What touches you so, my love?"

He lifted the hand to his lips. "You're a remarkable woman."

"No, I'm just ordinary old me." She smiled at him. "But I love you and I want you to be happy. That matters to me more than anything in the world. I'll dedicate my life to making you happy, Jake."

Jake sniffed again. "Me too, my love."

She lay her head against his chest and he kissed her hair. At long last they resumed their walk and Jake farewelled her at her bedroom door.

* * * *

"Is Lydia coming for supper tonight?"

"Of course, Ma. I'll go and fetch her right after school."

"I'm glad. I really like her, Son. I'm so proud of you both, I'm thrilled this has worked out for you."

"Me too." Jake grinned. "I couldn't be happier."

"I can tell by the light in your eyes." She put a hand on his shoulder.

"She loves you so much, Ma. She never knew her own mother and she told me she's thrilled to have a mother in her life at last."

Elsie embraced her son and kissed his cheek. "I'm pleased. Between her and Vi, I get to have two wonderful daughters. I'm delighted." She became serious then. "Are you sure you want me to stay here with you both when you marry? I could move to the boarding house. You deserve to have your own home."

"It is my own home, Ma, and we both want you here. You virtually have your own wing, anyway."

"Thank you, Jake."

"I better get going. I have to relieve Jarr."

"Okay, Son. When you go to town, I need a few groceries for the engagement party I'm hosting tomorrow night." She grinned. "Do you mind?"

"Course not. I'll swing by and get your list before I leave."

"Thank you, Son."

He winked at her and hurried out the door.

*   *   *   *

Jarrod stood and banged a fork against his glass to silence the crowd. "Welcome everyone to the Triple J Ranch. We're here to celebrate my brother and his lovely fiancée. Please refresh your glasses for the toast." Elsie and two of the town's women hurried around refilling glasses, while Jarrod continued. He gripped his brother's shoulder. "We're all thrilled for you both. I couldn't have asked for a better girl to welcome as a new sister." He kissed Lydia's cheek.

"Thank you, Jarrod." Lydia smiled at him.

"Ladies and Gentlemen, please raise your glasses to Jake and Lydia."

"Jake and Lydia," the crowd called out.

Jake raised his glass to Lydia and winked at her, as the gathered friends cheered. He kissed her deeply; the cheers continued so he prolonged the kiss. He stepped back and lifted his hand to get the attention of the crowd.

"I'd like to say something if I may. Thanks for celebrating with us." He turned to take Lydia's hand. "And I want to thank you, Lydia, for saying yes to me. I can't wait for us to spend our life together. I love you so much." He leaned in and kissed her again then turned back to the crowd. "We plan to get married in the New Year, after my new niece or nephew arrives." He grinned at his brother and Vi seated on the sofa nearby. He nodded. "And finally, I want to say thanks to Ma for..." The door opened and he lifted his eyes to the late-comers. All the color drained from his face. "What...?" His mouth hung open and his eyes grew wide. All heads turned to look at the older man and younger woman standing in the doorway.

"Hello." She smiled and looked around. "What's going on here?"

Lydia looked at Jake and frowned. He looked like he'd seen a ghost.

Elsie gasped. "Chrissy?"

Lydia's mouth dropped open. "That's Chrissy?"

A wide grin crossed Jake's face and almost by habit, he ran and wrapped his arms around her and lifted her off the ground. "What are you doing here?" Overwhelming feelings swept through him so intensely he nearly collapsed. He put her back on her feet and gripped her shoulder. "Chrissy, what're you doing here?"

"The case is closed; the men are in prison. They said we could go home." She gestured to her father.

Jake grinned. "I can't believe it. I thought I'd never see you again." His eyes sparkled as he shook her father's hand.

"No." He heard Lydia sob, and she hurried out of the room, hiding her face.

"Ohhhhh." Jake hung his head. Elsie left to follow Lydia.

115

Chrissy noticed the look of confusion and fear on Jake's face. She looked to where Lydia had run to, and to the gathered crowd then back to Jake. She screwed up her face. "What's going on? What is all this?"

Jake was frozen and far too overwhelmed to speak.

Jarrod approached. "It's an engagement party."

Chrissy frowned. "Who's?"

"Mine," Jake managed in a quiet voice.

"What do you mean?" Chrissy curled up her face. "How can you have an engagement party, who are you engaged to?"

"Lydia Howard, she's the new teacher here." Jake couldn't help but smile. Then he frowned as he looked at Chrissy's face.

"What? How can you be engaged? You're supposed to be engaged to me, remember?"

Jake shrugged and looked around at the crowd. This wasn't a conversation he wanted to have in front of everyone. All eyes were fixed on them and the people began to murmur.

"You mean you're engaged to two women at the same time?" Ian Cooper asked loudly, and the gathered crowd murmured amongst themselves.

Jake could do nothing but shrug. "I, I... I dunno..." he stammered.

"People, I think we should get out of here. Jake has some things he needs to sort out. Let's leave them to it," Eli called to the crowd and they began to disperse. He turned to Jake. "You want me to stay?"

Jake merely shook his head.

"Okay, you know where I am if you need me. I pray you can make sense of all this." Eli grimaced, praying fervently that hearts weren't about to be broken.

Jake nodded again and murmured his goodbyes to the departing neighbors. Jarrod gripped his shoulder and led his wife away.

Jake said nothing further until he and Chrissy were alone in the room. Her father had slipped out to tend to the horses.

"It's so good to see you, Jake. I've missed you so." Chrissy put her hand on his chest.

"I've missed you, too." Jake's voice trembled. His entire body was on fire. The feelings crashing through him were so strong he gripped the table to keep himself from collapsing. He looked at her face and his heart lurched. He lunged for her and wrapped her in his arms. "Chrissy." Tears ran down his cheeks. "Oh, Chrissy." He cradled her head in his hands, then pulled back from her. He looked her in the eye and without thinking he gave in to the overwhelming urge to kiss her. He kissed her deeply and pulling away from her, he lay his forehead against hers.

Elsie found Lydia in the guest bedroom lying on the bed, sobbing. "Lydia." She sat down next to the girl.

Lydia sat up and swiped at her eyes.

Elsie put her arm around her. "It'll be okay."

"Will it?" She spoke through her tears. "I saw how he looked at her."

"Darling, it was just the shock of seeing her again. He never got to say goodbye to her. I'm sure it's dragged up many feelings for him."

Lydia nodded. "What if he still loves her?"

"I'm sure in some ways he does, when you love someone it doesn't just go away. He'll need time to deal with those feelings. But he loves you fiercely, remember that?"

"What if he loves her more, and I'm just the second choice?"

"That's not going to happen. He loves you."

"And I love him, more than I ever thought possible." She began to sob again as she felt her heart shatter. This was worse agony than when Wyatt had betrayed her because she'd never really loved Wyatt. She felt like a knife was stabbing into her heart.

Elsie put her arms around her. "Darling, it'll be alright. You'll see. We need to pray about it." She had no idea how to help the young woman and her own foreboding feeling grew. She knew Jake loved Lydia and she'd grown to love the young woman as a daughter, more so than she ever had with Chrissy. But she knew that Jake had loved Chrissy deeply, too.

Lydia sat up and dried her eyes. "I think I'll go back to the boarding house so I can think and pray."

"Okay, I'll have Jarrod take you."

"Thank you, Mrs. Jenkins."

Elsie brushed some hair off the younger woman's face and kissed her forehead. "You're welcome, Dear. I'll be praying for you, both."

Lydia gave her a sad smile and both women stood. Elsie followed her out to the living room arriving in time to see Jake kissing Chrissy.

"Ohhhhhh." Lydia thrust both hands over her face and then hurried out the door.

Jake snapped his head up. "Lydia?" His heart was splitting in half. He followed her out the door and called out, "Lydia." But she was running through the snow toward town. "Lydia," he called louder but she didn't stop.

"Oh, Lord." Jake had no other words and he fell to his knees on the wide porch and buried his face in his hands. "Oh, Lord," he cried out and sat back on his feet.

Chrissy smirked and then abruptly sobered when she noticed Elsie looking at her. She plastered on a wry smile and followed Jake out. She knelt next to him and put her arms around him. He clung to her. Elsie shook her head and whispered a prayer for all the hearts that were involved and the unfortunate timing of all this. She hurried over to get Jarrod, so he could chase Lydia down and make sure she got home safely. It was a long way, and the new fallen snow was deep.

She arrived back to find Jake sitting on the sofa in the living room with Chrissy next to him.

"What's happening?" Jake managed. "What's going on?"

"Jake. I love you. I've never stopped loving you. I wanted to write, I tried so many times, but I wasn't allowed to. It was for your safety and mine."

Jake stared at his boots and swallowed over and over again. "Getting over you has been the hardest thing I've ever had to do."

"I'm so sorry." She leaned against him and gripped his arm. "I had no choice."

Jake nodded.

"I still love you," she said again. "Do you love me?"

"Chrissy, I..."

"I know you do, Jake, that kiss said you do."

"Chrissy, I..." there were no words to express the agonizing feelings.

"You love me don't you?" she persisted.

Jake could do nothing more than nod.

Chrissy grinned. "Then we can have a second chance. We can get married like we always planned to."

"But Lydia..."

"What about her? You were engaged to me first. We're still engaged. We never broke it off."

"You've been gone two and a half years..."

"That doesn't mean I stopped loving you and I know you still love me."

Jake shrugged. This morning he was deeply in love with Lydia and Chrissy was nothing more than a distant memory. But now seeing her, the feelings bubbled up again. But when he thought about Lydia... "Ohhhh." He gripped his temples and closed his eyes tightly.

Elsie entered the room. "Chrissy, I think you should go and let Jake work this out."

Chrissy frowned. "But, Mrs. Jenkins, He needs me."

"No, he needs time to think. We'll be here for him."

"But..." she tried to argue.

"Chrissy, if you really love him, you'll leave him to work this out."

A scowl crossed Chrissy's face for just a second, then she gave Elsie a wide smile and batted her eyelids. "Very well. I'll be at my brother's house on our old farm. That's where we're staying." She leaned across and kissed Jake's temple. "I'll see you tomorrow, my darling. I'm so glad we're home and I can't wait to start our life together again."

Jake said nothing. He buried his face in his hands and broke down in tears as the overwhelming feelings got the better of him.

Chrissy slunk out of the room with a scowl on her face, and hurried toward the barn to find her father.

*   *   *   *

"Lydia." Jarrod pulled the horse to a stop. "Lydia, stop." He leaped off the horse and reached out to stop her.

"Leave me be." Lydia sobbed.

"Lydia." Jarrod's voice was kind, he gently touched her arm. "You'll never make it back in this weather. It's a three mile walk."

"Ohhh." She burst into tears and Jarrod embraced her. "Come on, you can come back to our home. Vi will take care of you."

Lydia nodded into his chest.

Jarrod brought the two women cups of hot tea and opted to leave them to talk.

The two women watched him leave and sipped at their tea.

"Lydia, I'm so sorry about all this." Viola-Jane squeezed her hand.

Lydia gave Vi a smile. "It's not your fault."

Vi squeezed her hand again and looked at her intensely. "It's not Jake's either. He didn't expect Chrissy to ever come back."

"I know that. What do I do now?"

"What do you mean?"

"Where will I go? What will I do? I have no money."

"What are you saying?"

"He won't want me anymore now that he has the love of his life back." Lydia dropped her head and sniffed.

Vi gripped Lydia's arm. "You're the love of his life. He'll remember that."

Lydia lifted her eyes to Vi. "How can you be sure? I saw how he looked at her. I saw him kiss her. I'm sure they'll pick up where they left off. They never broke up, she just left and he never got closure."

"Exactly. What he needs is closure with her. Then he'll remember what he has with you and he'll never look back."

"How can you be sure of that, Vi?"

"I can't be for certain. All I know is that he's fiercely in love with you."

"But he was in love with her too. I know he loved her very much."

"I wasn't with Jarrod then, but I remember Chrissy and Jake. Yes he loved her, but not the way he loves you. Since you first came to town he's fought for you all the way. He saved you from Wyatt. He's loved you from the first day he saw you. I've never seen a man love the way he loves you."

"Oh, Vi. I love him so. I really do."

"Then you have to trust God with this. He's got it all in hand."

Lydia took a deep breath. "You're right. God has this in hand. I love Jake, with all my heart and I have to give him up to God."

"What do you mean?"

"I mean I love him so much that I want his happiness above all. And if it's Chrissy that makes him happy…" Her tears overflowed again and her lips began to quiver. "Then I have to let him go."

Vi bit her lip and squeezed Lydia's hand again. "I'm sorry. For what it's worth. Jarrod and I will be here for both of you."

Lydia smiled through her tears. "Thank you. You've been a good friend."

"And we always will be. We're on your side."

"Vi, it's not a competition. I want what's best for Jake. I truly do." She sobbed. "Even if that's not me." Her voice was barely above a whisper.

"You're a brave girl, Lydia."

"I have to trust God with Jake."

Vi squeezed her hand again and nodded. "You can stay here as long as you like."

"Thank you. But I need to get back to the boarding house, I have school on Monday."

"Well at least stay and finish your tea. I'll have Jarrod drive you home when you're ready."

* * * *

Jake had his head in his hands when Jarrod walked in. He sat down next to his brother and squeezed his shoulder. "Jake."

Jake sighed, swiped at his eyes with his sleeve and looked at his brother.

"I just want you to know, Lydia is with Vi at our home."

"Good." Jake swallowed and sighed.

"I'm sorry about all this."

Jake shrugged.

"What're you going to do?"

"What can I do? Somehow I'm engaged to two women at the same time. I never expected to ever see Chrissy again." He shrugged.

Jarrod squeezed his brother's shoulder again. "Do you still love her?"

Jake shrugged. "I didn't think I did."

"Until you saw her again?"

Jake nodded.

"And Lydia?"

"I love her so much, but I've lost her now haven't I?" Jake sighed and hung his head.

"I'm not so sure about that."

"She saw me kiss Chrissy. I'm not sure why I did, it was an impulse I suppose."

Jarrod nodded. "Yeah."

Jake exhaled loudly.

"You have some thinking and praying to do, Jake. We'll be praying for you too."

"Thank you." Jake's voice was raspy and full of emotion. "Any advice?" He smirked.

Jarrod gave his brother a wry smile. "No, except be honest with them both. Pray a lot, and don't make any promises until you're certain."

"I don't want to hurt either of them."

"Well, hurt is rather inevitable in this situation, I'm afraid. All three of you stand to face hurt. All you can do is minimize the amount by being honest, and not hiding anything from either of them."

Jake nodded. "Thanks, Brother. And thanks for looking out for Lydia."

Jarrod squeezed his shoulder. "Of course. We love her too."

"And Chrissy?"

"Jake, if Chrissy is the one who's going to make you happy, we'll love her, of course. We want you to be happy."

"Thank you." Jake took a deep breath. "I should go and see Lydia, make sure she's okay."

"Sure, she's at my place. Come on."

Jake took another deep breath and stood up.

*　*　*　*

"Lydia." Jake entered the living room.

Lydia looked up and swallowed, her mismatched eyes were fill with tears and her face curled up with pain. Not unlike when he'd found her after Wyatt had betrayed her.

Viola stood. "I'll leave you to it."

Lydia smiled her thanks to Viola.

Jake sat down next to Lydia, he lifted a hand to brush away her tears. "I'm so sorry."

Lydia gave him a brave smile. "It's not your fault."

"No, but you're hurting and I hate that you are." He closed his eyes and sighed.

"Jake, I understand. It must be so confusing having her come back out of the blue like that."

Jake turned to look at Lydia. "I do love you, you know, very much and I don't want to hurt you."

"I saw you kiss her."

Jake closed his eyes and trembled. "I'm sorry."

Lydia swallowed and took a deep breath, she looked Jake in the eye. "You love her don't you?"

Jarrod's words echoed in his head *be honest with her.* "Yes, I think I still do. I didn't know that I did, until I saw her and everything came bubbling up. We've been sweethearts since I was fifteen."

Lydia's tears escaped. "But you love me too?"

Jake took her hand. "More than I can put into words."

"How can you love two women at the same time?"

"Because I love you differently. You're very different women."

"And you loved her first."

Jake nodded.

"And you love her more than me, don't you?"

Jake gripped Lydia's hand. "No. Not more, just differently. I thought you had completely replaced Chrissy in my heart, and I never expected to see her again." He sighed. "I want to be honest with you, I don't want there to be any secrets between us. No sneakiness. You deserve that much."

She nodded.

"If she hadn't left we'd've been married for more than two years by now."

Lydia nodded again; her eyes never left his face.

"Seeing her again, all those overwhelming feelings came bubbling up. That hug and kiss was just an old impulse. I'm sorry I betrayed you." He sucked in a tear and dropped his head.

Lydia lifted his chin. "You didn't betray me. You're a man and you find yourself in a very confusing situation." She raised a hand to his cheek. "I appreciate your honesty. Can I be honest with you too?"

"Please." Jake's voice shook. He took the hand from his face and held it.

"Jake, I love you. I love you so very much. You saved me from an awful situation and you've been nothing but kind and loving to me since I arrived in town. You're a wonderful man and that hasn't changed. I don't envy you the situation you find yourself in." She smiled at him and placed her spare hand on his chest. "But I need to give you up."

Jake's face curled up in pain. "What're you saying, you want to break our engagement?"

She smiled and put her hand back on his cheek. "No, I want to marry you. I love so much. But more than that, I want you to be happy. Your happiness means everything to me. And if it's Chrissy that makes you happy." She sighed and her eyes flooded with tears. "Then I want that for you." Her voice trembled and a sob escaped her. She slipped her engagement ring from her finger and passed it to him. "I release you from our engagement."

Tears rolled down Jake's cheeks. His heart was breaking. "Lydia. I love you so much, I'm sorry about all this."

"I know. And I love you. I'll always love you. But you need to go and work out who is going to make you happy." She kissed his cheek.

"What about you?" He sobbed.

"I'll be here, loving you, no matter what. And when you're ready to make your choice, I'll support you, no matter who you choose." She closed her eyes. Her heart didn't feel as confident as her words sounded.

Jake broke down in tears and buried his face in his hands.

Lydia put her arms around him and held him.

"I'm so sorry," he whimpered. "I'm so sorry. I don't wanna hurt you."

"Hey..." She kissed his forehead. "I don't want to see you hurting either."

He sat back and cupped her cheek. "I do love you, very much."

She nodded. "Promise me you'll give it a lot of thought and prayer and you'll make the decision that will make you happy, that's what I want. Truly, Jake. I just want you to be happy."

He nodded.

"Promise me. Your happiness is more important to me than my broken heart." She sobbed, drawing strength from the Lord.

He brushed a tear from her cheek. "Thank you." He stood and gestured for Lydia to stand and wrapped his arms around her. "I promise. I will not make you wait longer than I need to. I need to spend some time in prayer."

"Yes you do," she murmured into his chest. "And I know in order to make this choice you will have to spend time with her. As much as I'll hate to see that, I understand."

"I'm sorry."

"No, don't be. I want you to be certain. So when you make your choice, I'll be here. And if you chose her, I'll go and live with my brother in Virginia. I couldn't bear to be here and not be able to be with you."

Jake could do nothing but nod. He leaned in and kissed her cheek. "You're a remarkable woman."

She nodded and smiled bravely. She was tiring of always being so brave.

Jake nodded to her again and walked out. He saddled Duke and went for a long ride around the range, spending the rest of the evening and late into the night in fervent prayer, in the cold, unforgiving wind.

Fourteen

"Jake." Chrissy grinned and threw her arms around him. "It's so wonderful to be in your arms again."
Jake returned her embrace. He had to admit it felt good to hold her again.

"Shall we eat?" He gestured to the table.

She nodded and he seated her and took the seat opposite her at the café. Hannah-Mae passed them a menu, gave Jake a sad smile and put a hand on his shoulder. The entire town was invested in Jake's situation. In the week since Chrissy came back to town he'd heard plenty of gossip about being engaged to two women. The towns people took sides. Some even kept a tally, making wagers about who he'd end up with. There were no secrets in a small town.

It was heart-wrenching for Jake, but he'd given Lydia his word, he'd be absolutely certain.

Eli had been a big help. He refused to take sides and prayed extensively with Jake.

"Before we go any further I want say a few things." Jake looked at Chrissy. She nodded. He reached for her hand. "Chrissy. I'm all kinds of confused right now. I never expected to ever see you again and Lydia and I are engaged. Well... it's on hold for now until I work out what I'm supposed to do. She's told me to be sure of what I want."

"What's there to be sure of? You and I are in love. We've been sweethearts a long time. I never stopped loving you."

"And I never stopped loving you."

"Then how could you get engaged to another woman?"

"Did you expect me to just sit here and pine for you forever?"

"No, but you must've known I'd be back."

"I didn't know what to think. You disappeared in the blink of an eye and I know it wasn't your fault, but it broke my heart. Now seeing you again? I don't know how to feel. But I do know I love Lydia very much and I don't want to hurt her."

"Well you're gonna have to hurt one of us."

He closed his eyes. "I hate that. I don't want anyone to get hurt."

"You've known me the longest. I don't understand why this is so hard for you. You've only been with her five minutes."

"Because I have to be certain."

"In the meantime we can court." She grinned.

"Yes. But I don't want to rub it in with Lydia so we need to keep it casual, I mean it's not fair on her if she has to see us hugging and kissing."

"So I can't court the man I love properly because of her." She spat the word her spitefully.

"Chrissy, how would you feel?"

Chrissy sighed. "Yeah alright. I'll take whatever I can get. But you have to make a decision soon. I've been without you for nearly three years and I want us to get married as soon as possible. I've waited all that time." She pouted.

Jake nodded. "Trust me. I want this to be sorted once and for all, just as much as you do."

Chrissy seethed internally. *Doesn't he know this is unfair to me? I'm suffering and he doesn't even seem to care.*

"So now can you tell me where you were?"

"New York City."

Jake's eyes widened. "That would've been a very different life for you and your father."

"Yeah, it took him a long time to adjust. He was grieving for Ma, he missed Mark and Tina and he struggled to adjust to the city."

"Where did he work?"

"The Marshall got him a job as a blacksmith."

"What did you do?"

"I went to finishing school for the first year. I was probably a wee bit old for it, but I learned a lot about city etiquette."

"I have to admit you look like a debutante, very sophisticated. You speak so fancy too. It seems like you adjusted well to the city."

"Yeah, but I like being back here. Although I admit I grew to love the city, and I made good friends there. I got a job in a clothing store, we sold beautiful gowns and hats. I enjoyed working." She tried to keep her voice light and even despite her growing frustration.

Hannah-Mae placed down their plates and Jake nodded his thanks. "It sounds like you fell on your feet. Did you have to change your names?"

"No, the outlaws would've known what I looked like but not my name. But it's easy to get lost in New York City, they could never find us there."

"And it's really all over?"

"Yes. The court case went on forever. It took a long time to catch them, but I was the first person they'd left alive and I was able to give a description of their looks and it made it easier to catch them in the long run."

"I'm glad you're free of them. It must've been scary."

"It was at first. I couldn't sleep well for months, I kept expecting the outlaws to burst through the door. Also I missed my mother and you." She squeezed his hand and batted her eyelids. "But at least, I knew you were alive."

They finished their meal and Jake walked Chrissy home. He kissed her cheek.

"Aren't you going to kiss me properly?"

"I don't think so, Chrissy. I'm not going to kiss Lydia either. I'll save my affection for the woman I chose to marry, it wouldn't be fair on either of you."

Chrissy tried to hide her frustration. She pouted and gave him a pitiful look. "Okay, I can wait till then. I love you, Jake."

He nodded.

"Don't you love me too?"

"Chrissy, I told you. I love you and I love Lydia. I just love you both differently. I have to work out what I need to do. Until then I'm going to save my affection."

Chrissy turned her head so he couldn't see her grit her teeth. "Very well." She plastered on a smile and turned back to him. She stood on her toes and kissed his cheek. "Goodnight."

"Goodnight." He smiled.

*   *   *   *

Jake stared blankly at the dancing flames and sipped at his coffee. Elsie finished wiping up and sat next to him. "How's it going, Son?"

He gave his mother a sad smile. "I'm just as confused as ever."

"It's been four weeks, you aren't any closer to a decision?"

"I wish I could say I was. Christmas is approaching and I want to be certain before then."

"I've been praying for you all."

Jake smiled. "I appreciate that, Ma."

"How's Lydia?"

"I spoke to her briefly today. She's very gracious, she wants me to be happy."

"And Chrissy?"

"She asks every day for an answer. But I'm enjoying spending time with her. I feel like I'm getting to know her again."

"She seems to have changed."

Jake nodded and smiled. "She's become a rather elegant woman. The city suited her, I guess."

Elsie nodded. *Why can't you see that Lydia is the girl for you? She's more suited to you than Chrissy ever was and she's sweet and wonderful. I never really trusted Chrissy. She always seemed a little hung up in her appearance.* His mother wanted to scream at him and shake him and make him see what he had in Lydia, but she wouldn't pry. He needed to work it out himself, do what made him happy. He would in time. "So are you ready for your trip?"

"Yeah, and I think it's good timing, it'll give me time away to think and pray."

"That might be for the best. How many days will you be gone this time?"

"Only two nights, it's a good time while the weather is clear and the snow isn't too thick. It takes nearly half a day to get to Grandvale with a wagon in tow, then it'll take a few days to get what I need and find a new buyer for the spring calves, now that old Thompson has passed."

"You'll find someone."

"Yeah, Jarr had a few contacts from his last trip."

"He won't go instead of you? You have a lot to work out."

"He offered, but no. I want to go. I need to be away from town and from both women. It'll do me some good."

"Well, I'll miss you, Son."

"If you give me your Christmas list I'll get what you need."

"Thank you, it would be nice to have some things from a larger town that we can't get around here."

"I want to do some Christmas shopping too."

"What time will you leave?"

"First light."

"Very good. I'll get up a list for you and leave it on the counter."

"Thanks, Ma. I'll turn in now. I love you, you know, no matter what happens, you'll always be my girl." He bent down to kiss her cheek.

"Away with you." She chuckled and stood to take the cups to the kitchen.

Fifteen

Lydia closed the school house door, picked up her basket and headed for town. She sighed as she walked down the shoveled path. "Lord, please bless Jake. Help him with this decision. And help me to accept his choice, no matter what it is." She swiped at a tear. "I love him very much, and I just want his happiness."

She needed to get a few things for school the next day, so she hurried back to her room, stowed her school books, grabbed her empty basket, and headed for the mercantile.

She gave the clerk a sad smile as she entered. He nodded to her and she hurried to the corner of the store, looking for chalk.

"Well if it isn't the schoolteacher?"

Lydia's head snapped up and she sucked in a sharp breath. "Good day, Miss Adams. I trust you're well?" She smiled as kindly as she could, despite the stabbing pain in her heart.

"I'll be better when Jake finally makes up his mind."

Lydia closed her eyes and tucked her lips under. She sniffed back the tears. "It's very difficult for him."

"I'm not sure why. We've been in love a long time. He just needs to be reminded of that, I guess. I sure wish he'd hurry up." Chrissy rolled her eyes and sighed dramatically.

"He needs to be certain of what he wants, and that will take time." Lydia's voice trembled. "I understand."

"You should just bow out and make the choice easier for yourself. He's going to chose me, obviously. Why don't you leave now and spare yourself the pain?"

A shudder ran through Lydia. She bit back three snarky retorts that entered her mind and sought strength from the Lord. She managed a smile. "I just want him to be happy. I'll be happy knowing he's happy."

Chrissy grinned. "He's happy with me. There's no question he'll choose me. We have so much history together."

Lydia nodded. "When that time comes, I'll be happy for him. I love him very much."

Chrissy grimaced and frowned. "I doubt you love him more than me."

"I love him more than I love myself. His happiness is what matters to me. I don't like watching him hurt. It breaks my heart." Lydia closed her eyes and sighed. "He deserves to be happy."

"Well I'm getting tired of waiting. He needs to make his choice soon, so we can get married." Chrissy thrust her hands on her hips.

Lydia nodded. There was little else she could do. "I'm praying for him. I pray every day that he'll work out what will make him happy."

Chrissy grimaced at Lydia.

"Now if you'll excuse me, I have some shopping to do. Good day, Miss Adams." Lydia turned and hurried away, desperately fighting the threatening tears. *Oh, Lord, please help me to stay strong and to accept Jake's choice, whatever is it. Bless him, and help him to make the choice that makes him happy. I love him so.* She swiped at a tear and drew her mind back to her shopping.

"Hmmmpf." Chrissy groaned, stamped her feet and snatched her basket off the floor to finish her own shopping. *I'm getting tired of waiting. He's obviously going to choose me. Why would he pick her? I can't understand why he loves her in the first place. She's so weird looking. Well, I'll remind him of what he's missing out on, and show him who the teacher really is, that'll make the choice easier for him.*

*   *   *   *

"What are you grinning at, Sister?"

Chrissy looked up at Mark as she waited for him to hitch the gig.

"I just have a plan."

"A plan?" Mark looked at her over the sorrell's back and raised his brows.

"To make sure I win Jake back from that woman."

Mark frowned. "There's no need to be unkind. It's not her fault."

Chrissy scowled. "No, but he needs to see that I'm the obvious choice."

Mark raised his brows again. "How so?"

Chrissy grinned...

*   *   *   *

Jake finished his task a day early and headed for home. He'd spent almost the entire trip praying and thinking. He found talking to the amphibians comforting. They didn't offer him any advice but they were good listeners. Speaking aloud to them helped him make sense of his choice.

The two women he found himself engaged to were both lovely in their own right. Several times he made a certain decision only to change it again. Chrissy had changed a lot, she had an air of city refinement about her now, but the woman he'd loved since he was a teenager was still there and his heart longed for her.

But, Lydia was the most intriguing woman he'd ever met. She was beautiful and interesting, kind and sweet.

Ahhh, but he'd known Chrissy longer, they had history, she was his first love.

He'd stayed up late in the night in the small boarding house and spent the night in prayer. He'd wrestled with it and thought about who he could see himself with in his future. In the small hours of the morning he finally made a decision. With a relived sigh he climbed into bed, hoping to get a few hours sleep.

Jake left early and smiled. Now that he'd made his choice, the horrible churning in his stomach and mind had stopped. He hated that he had to hurt one of them, and he knew it would break her heart but he couldn't help that and he knew in the long run he had no choice. He'd already made her wait a month and that was long enough. He'd let her down as kindly as he could. She'd be upset, but she was strong and he knew in the long term she'd be okay.

He drove into the ranch around midday, greeted his mother, unpacked the supplies and enjoyed lunch with her.

He wiped his mouth and pushed his plate back. "I need to go to town, Ma."

"But you just got home?"

"I need to talk to Jack Easton, he wanted me to pick up some supplies urgently. I'll drop them off and then go and surprise Chrissy. I have a gift for her from the city."

Elsie nodded. The wry smile on his face prompted her to ask, "Any closer to making a decision, Son?"

He nodded and smiled. "I think so. I've spent some time thinking and praying and I think God is leading in one direction."

"Might I know your thoughts?"

He grinned and kissed his mother's cheek. "You'll know soon enough." He winked at her and hurried out the door.

Elsie shook her head. *Lord, I pray he makes the right choice. I only want his happiness.* She'd been praying that a lot lately.

* * * *

Jake approached the Adams farm. He had a bottle of Chrissy's favorite perfume and a new hair comb. He was almost certain that she was the one. God had brought her back into his life for a reason and he didn't believe in coincidences.

He couldn't help but feel heart-broken about hurting lovely Lydia, but he'd loved Chrissy since he was fifteen. She'd been the joy of his heart for a long time. He hitched Duke to a post near the house and walked toward the front door. He hesitated when he noticed the barn across the way was open and he heard voices. One sounded like Chrissy, but he couldn't be sure, so he walked closer and listened.

Jake grinned and took a step toward the barn, to surprise her with his gifts, and his choice. He heard his name and paused to listen.

"...we've been sweethearts since our school days."

"I know. But a lot has happened since then," Mark replied.

"So, we can still pick up where we left off."

Jake grinned. "Maybe we can." He was just about to head in when he heard Mark's words. He paused again.

"Have you told him about Walter?"

"No. He doesn't need to know."

Jake frowned and held his breath, a rising feeling of foreboding grew in him.

"That you were engaged to him pretty well the whole time you were in New York and you only came back because he dropped you? Of course Jake needs to know. Secrets don't stay hidden. Even New York City breaks its silence, eventually."

"I'll tell him after we're married. Then it'll be too late and besides, it doesn't matter."

Jake grimaced and furrowed his brows. This was starting to feel a lot like Wyatt McCain all over again.

"Why do you still want to marry him?"

"He's half owner of that ranch, there's a lot of money in that. We lived well in New York, and I need to maintain that lifestyle."

Jake's brows flew up. His blood began to boil. He got the feeling he was being manipulated. He thought about storming in, but he was intrigued to find out what she was planning. Clearly, she wasn't who he thought she was after all. Three years can really change a person.

"So you just want him for his money?" Mark scowled as he tightened the last buckle.

"Well, he's handsome too. I could do a lot worse."

"Do you still love him?"

Chrissy shrugged. "I don't hate him. I don't have the feelings for him that I had for Walter, but at least I like Jake. He's handsome and the wealthiest rancher in town. He's a good enough choice, there isn't anyone else in this town I'd want to be with."

"Chrissy, are you sure you want to do this?"

"Of course, I think we can be happy together, eventually. I'm a better choice than SHE is." Chrissy spat the word she.

Mark shook his head. "So, what is this grand plan?"

She sneered. "I'm going to make him see that she can't be trusted."

"And how are you going to do that?" Mark frowned. His sister had really changed and frankly, he wasn't impressed with who she'd become. Their father had told him that she'd become snobbish and rather unkind in the city. She'd got in with a wealthy lot at finishing school and it had affected her for the worse.

"Since I work at the post office I've got a friend to send a letter to Lydia, as though from a lover. I'll intercept it and give it to Jake. He'll see her for who she really is, and he'll be mine. We'll marry right away and I'll move into the house on the ranch. I can see myself in that big house. It's one of the nicest and largest in the town. They've done very well for themselves. Of course we'll have to get his mother to move out. She'll just be in the way…"

Jake gasped and seethed. How could she do that? And to try to make him doubt Lydia… he'd heard enough. He threw the perfume and the hair comb in the snow, leapt up on Duke and headed out.

Mark shook his head. "Are you sure you want to win him through manipulation and trickery? Is that what you want to base a marriage on?"

"He'll never know, and he loves me, so I know it's only a matter of time. I'm just speeding up the process. Might as well put that woman out of her misery. Honestly, I don't see what he sees in her. Her eyes are weird. Have you ever seen a person with two different colored eyes like that?"

"No, but she seems nice enough." Mark shrugged.

"You wouldn't know. Now can you hurry with the gig? I need to get into town to intercept the post." She grinned.

Mark walked the horse and gig out and helped her up into it, shaking his head as she drove away. He turned to walk back to the barn, when something shining in the snow caught his eye. He walked over and picked up the perfume and hair comb. He turned it over in his hand and frowned. "I wonder where these came from?"

He looked around at the yard but there were no signs of someone being there, but then he had just shoveled all the snow away from the path, so there was no trace. He shrugged and walked back into the house. Perhaps Chrissy had dropped them.

*　*　*　*

Jake walked out of the post office and slipped the envelope in his pocket. He shook his head and seethed internally. "Thank you, Lord, for allowing me to be in the right place at the right time and to avoid making the biggest mistake of my life." It had taken some persuading to get Arthur to give him the letter, since it wasn't addressed to him but when Jake had told him what he'd overheard, the man had been happy to oblige. Jake made him promise he wouldn't tell Chrissy he had the letter. He made a few purchases while he was in town, then headed to the café to meet Chrissy as he'd previously arranged.

*   *   *   *

Jake stood up as Chrissy entered the café.

"Sorry I'm late, Jake, thanks for waiting for me."

"That's okay." He smiled and pulled the chair out for her.

Chrissy noticed the gleam in Jake's eye. "You look happy?"

"Just enjoyed my trip is all."

"Well I'm glad you're back. I missed you very much."

"I missed you too." He smiled as kindly as he could as they waited for Hannah-Mae.

Chrissy sighed loudly and frowned.

Jake took her hand. "Hey, What's the matter?"

"Oh, it's nothing really. I was just expecting something to arrive and it hasn't come. I can't understand it."

"You know the post is often late?"

She frowned. "I never said it was the post."

Jake shrugged. "I just assumed. Was it on the stage?" He covered himself.

"No, it should've been in today's post. The stage delivered the mail this morning." She smiled.

"Oh, I'm sorry it didn't arrive." Jake tried to sound nonchalant, but he seethed internally. "Who was it from?"

"A friend from the city. I haven't seen her since we got back and we're planning a visit in the new year. She was writing to catch me up on all the news since I've been gone."

Jake nodded. He shook his head slightly at Hannah-Mae and the woman gave him a nod and hurried away to another table.

Chrissy frowned. "Why did you send her away?"

Jake sighed loudly. He could bear it no longer. "Because I won't eat with a woman who would manipulate me to get her own way."

Chrissy's face flushed. "What? What're you saying? I love you, Jake. I've always loved you."

Jake shook his head sadly. "No you don't."

Chrissy put her hand on his arm. "Jake, what's the matter. I thought you loved me."

"I thought I did too, but I realise now that I don't even know who you are anymore."

"What? Jake. What're you talking about?"

He stood up, pulled a brown envelope from his pocket and slid it across the table to her. He tapped his finger on it twice and looked her in the eye. "Thank you for making the choice so easy for me." He turned and walked away.

Chrissy looked from his steely gaze to the envelope. Recognising the return address, she gasped and dropped her eyes. "Jake, wait, it's not what it seems," she called to his retreating figure. Running to chase him out the door. "Jake." She grabbed his arm. "This is just a letter from an old friend. Why would you be so upset?"

He spun around on the boardwalk as the door slammed shut behind her. "I am not your cashcow." He furrowed his brow. "I heard what you said in the barn to your brother, and your manipulation is over." He grimaced and sighed. *I hope Lydia will forgive me.*

Chrissy stamped her feet and thrust her arms across her chest. "Jake," she yelled. "Jake, we can fix this. I promise I love you. It's just a misunderstanding." But he ignored her and kept on walking.

Chrissy chased him and put her hand on his shoulder. "Please, Jake."

Jake paused. "Chrissy, leave me be, I need to think." His voice was tight and raspy.

Chrissy pouted and groaned, scowling as he walked away.

* * * *

Jake took a deep breath and knocked on the door.
"Who is it?"
"Jake."
"Just a minute." Lydia gasped and let out a sob. "Lord, help me to be strong." She shuddered, she knew what was about to come. She'd dreaded this moment since she'd seen Jake seated in the café with Chrissy, holding her hand. Seeing them together broke her heart. She'd been praying a lot lately, drawing on the Lord for her strength. "I guess I

should be glad that he's not making me wait any longer, Lord. It's been agonising." She glanced across at her brother's letter sitting on her small cabinet. He'd agreed that she could come and live with him. She took a deep breath, plastered on her smile, and opened the door. "Hello." She gave him a sad smile. Jake looked nervous and fidgety. He had a deep furrow to his brow, and he swallowed over and over.

"Do you want to come in?" Lydia tried desperately to keep her tears from falling.

Jake swallowed again. "Actually, I was wondering if you'd take a walk with me?"

She nodded. "Let me get my coat?" She reached across and flicked it off the hook.

"Let me help you with that," he offered, his voice shaky with emotion.

She nodded and allowed him to help her. His hands shook and she could hear his rapid breaths as he was trying to keep his emotions steady. She closed her eyes for a moment and curled her lips under. *Lord, this is torture. Please give me strength.* She exhaled and turned with a sad smile. "Where do you want to go?"

"It's cold out, I thought maybe the church, it's warm and private." He raised his brows and his lips quivered.

She nodded. Maybe she could stay and pray for a time afterward. She would need the Lord's help to get over him.

Jake offered her his arm and she took it. *Even now he's so kind.* She sighed. *I'm really going to miss his gentle care.* They walked in silence until they were inside the church. Jake took her coat, hung it on the hook, and added two pieces of wood to the stove. She sat down on the side of the nearest pew. He stood, turned around to look at her, and exhaled loudly. "Lydia..." He stopped.

"Jake." She stood up and her tears flowed. "I know what you've come to say and I told you I'd understand. I just want you to be happy." She blinked away the tears.

"I hope I will be."

"I hope that, too. I really do. I'll always love you, Jake. I have no hard feelings, I understand. Truly." Her lips quivered and her extraordinary eyes flooded with tears. She was trying to be brave but she wasn't able to keep the emotion at bay.

Jake closed his eyes and shook his head. *How could I have even considered Chrissy when the most gracious and loving woman I've ever met is here before me? Lord I pray she'll have me back, though I don't deserve her.*

He opened his eyes and they glistened with tears. "You're a remarkable woman. You're so gracious and kind, even when I know you've been hurting."

"I'm nothing special. I just trust God with my future." She smiled through her tears. "And yours."

Jake reached up and cupped her cheek. "I'm so sorry I've hurt you all these weeks."

She swallowed and blinked back the tears. "It's okay, I told you to be sure. I won't be anyone's second choice. I understand; you and Chrissy have loved each other since you were school children." *This is agonising, why won't he just put me out of my misery?* "Please, just say what you have to say. I can't bear this any longer." Her tears increased.

He nodded and turned his back and took two steps away. *Thy will be done, Lord. If she refuses me it's only what I deserve.* He let out a single sob then swallowed it back and turned around.

Lydia closed her eyes tightly and waited for the words to come. Jake knelt before her. She snapped her eyes open as she felt him reach for her hand. She gasped. "Jake?"

He was holding the ring out to her, his hands visibly shaking and tears streaming from his cheeks. "Lydia." He sniffed. "Would you forgive me?" A sob escaped his lips. "I love you so much. I know I've hurt you, and I don't deserve your forgiveness." Another sob and another sniff. "Is there a chance you'll agree to be my wife. It's been you all along, you're the one who's loved me and never wavered. You're the one who graciously supported me no matter what choice I made, at the risk of your own heart and happiness. I never should've hesitated for even a moment." He sniffed again as his tears increased.

Lydia burst into tears. She took her hand from him, stood, and walked over to look at the stove, she put her hands over her face and sobbed out all the overwhelming feelings from the last, agonising month.

Jake hung his head and sat back on his feet. He dropped the ring box to the floor and covered his face with his hands. Deep hulking sobs rocked him. *Lord,*

I can't believe I've ruined this. I can't believe I've blown my chance with her.

Lydia took a deep breath and wiped her eyes. She walked back to Jake and knelt in front of him. She picked up the ring box and put her hand on his shoulder. He opened his eyes and sucked back the tears. He expected to see anger and hurt in her eyes.

Instead she smiled at him. Lifted the ring out of the box and slid it on her finger. "Of course, Jake. Of course, I'll marry you."

Jake looked at her, his mouth fell open and slowly turned to a wide smile. He let out a strained sob and looked at her, quite unable to believe what was happening. His heart was doing somersaults. It had expected to be torn out, instead, it was bubbling over with joy.

Lydia lifted a hand to his cheek and her beautiful eyes explored his face. She smiled broadly. "I love you, Jake Jenkins."

He sucked in a breath, took the hand from his face, and kissed it. He wrapped his arms around her and stood, lifting her up with him. He spun her around and she threw her arms around his neck.

He kissed her deeply and then lay his forehead against hers. Tears ran down his cheeks. "Lydia. Oh. I can't believe you'd give me a second chance."

"Of course, Jake. I love you. I'll always love you."

"I'm so sorry I hurt you. I'm so sorry, my love. It was always you, always! I should never've doubted that for even a moment."

Lydia became very serious, she cupped both of his cheeks and smiled at him. "Jake, don't be sorry. I'm not glad this happened, but I'm happy, because I know for sure that you're certain and that you've chosen me rather than settled for me."

Jake smiled for the first time. "I'd choose you a thousand times a day. I'm sorry this happened but I've never been so certain of anything in all my life. I can't wait to spend my life with you, and I don't want to wait. I want to marry you tomorrow."

She smiled slowly. "Tomorrow?"

"Yes, I don't ever want to be without you ever again."

"Oh, Jake."

He lifted her into his arms and walked across to a pew. He sat down and pulled her onto his knee into his arms. She lay her head against his. "It feels so good to be in your arms again. I've missed it so much."

"My arms have ached for you."

She grimaced. "You would've filled them with Chrissy instead."

"No. Apart from that one kiss you saw I never embraced or kissed her again, except on the cheek."

"Really, why?"

"Because I didn't want to kiss or embrace either of you until I was sure you'd be the only one I ever kissed or embraced ever again. I'm sorry that I kissed Chrissy." He tucked some hair behind her ear. "I'm sorry you had to see my weakness like that. I know now it was just the confused feelings coming back up. Chrissy is not the woman she used to be and to marry

153

her instead of you would've been the biggest mistake of my life. I'm so grateful to God that I worked it out before it was too late."

"I was so sure you'd chosen her, given all your history."

"I sure am glad I didn't." He grinned and kissed her again. "I've absolutely made the right choice."

"Ohh, Jake, I'm so happy. Do you really want to get married tomorrow?"

"Mmmhmm, after the church service. We'll surprise everyone."

She grinned. "I'd like that, I can't wait to be your wife." She frowned. "Oh, but I don't have a special dress."

He stroked her cheek. "I don't care about that. You're beautiful just as you are. You could wear a flour sack and I'd still think you were incredibly beautiful."

"Oh, Jake." She kissed him again.

Sixteen

"You're far away, Son."

Jake turned his eyes from the amphibians and nodded. He'd worked hard to keep the wry grin off his face all morning, lest he spoil the surprise. He couldn't believe he'd be bringing his wife home with him that very night. "Yeah, just got a lot on my mind."

"I understand." Elsie gripped his arm. "You look nice today. That's your good suit, isn't it?"

"Yeah." He nodded.

"You don't normally wear it to church."

"I thought it might make me feel a little more confident if I dressed up."

"Well you look right handsome, Son. Whichever of those ladies you choose will be blessed indeed." *I sure hope its Lydia. I can't think of a better woman for him.*

Jake determinedly kept the grin from his face. Instead he changed the subject and made small talk with his mother.

Never had Jake been so distracted in church in all his life. He was certain it was the longest service in history. Lydia sat three rows in front of him in her lovely green gown, her red hair hung long down her back. How he longed for her. His arms actually ached for her. Now that he knew without a doubt she was the woman for him, he never wanted to be without her ever again.

Chrissy sat in the corner with her father and brother, with a tight scowl on her face. Jake grimaced.

He hated that she was hurting, but he wasn't sorry about his choice. He couldn't believe he'd very nearly chosen a woman who was prepared to manipulate him like that. *Thank you, Lord, for saving me from a lifetime of misery.* He'd been awake most of the night and he'd come to the conclusion that it was always Lydia. That he'd thought to choose Chrissy mostly out of obligation and the wonder at what he'd missed out on. But now there was absolutely no doubt, the thought of spending the rest of his life with Lydia thrilled him to the core. In some ways he was glad God had brought Chrissy back into his life, because he knew he was finally free of her, once and for all. It was Lydia who occupied every inch of his heart. He would no longer have to worry about the 'what ifs'.

At long last, the service finished. The pastor prayed a benediction over the congregation. People rose and began to leave, but he raised his hands to quiet them.

"Before you all leave," he thundered over the chatter. "Folks, please return to your seats. The service isn't quite finished." He grinned.

Heads turned and murmurs began as the people regained their seats and looked around at each other attempting to work out what was happening. Jake grinned and his mother squinted at him.

"Jake Jenkins, would you come to the front please?"

Elsie gave him a sideways smile and Jarrod and Eli both raised their brows. Jake grinned at them, kissed his mother's forehead, and walked to the front.

He nodded to the pastor; turned to the congregation and his eyes fell to Lydia's. A wide grin crossed his face. "Everyone, if you could stay for a few more minutes, I have a surprise for you." He paused and swiped at his eyes. "There's going to be a wedding." His face beamed.

Chrissy growled loudly, stood, and ran from the room.

Elsie gasped and her eyes lit up. "Really, Son?"

"Really, Ma." He put a hand out to his bride. "Lydia?"

She stood and walked to him and took his hand.

"Ohhhhhh, Son." Elsie began to weep, tears of overwhelming joy. Jarrod grinned and Eli jumped up and ran to the front. Jake frowned at him.

"It's okay, I'm not objecting, I just want to return the favor."

Jake embraced his friend.

"I couldn't be more thrilled for you Jake." Eli whispered and patted his friends back

Sylvia followed to stand with Lydia. She embraced the younger woman. "I'm so happy for you both." She whispered in Lydia's ear.

The pastor gripped Jake's shoulder. The two men nodded to each other. Jake turned and took Lydia's hands in his and looked into her remarkable eyes.

The pastor began. "Dearly beloved..."

The wide grin on Jake's face didn't leave for the entire ceremony. He looked into those amazing mismatched eyes and couldn't believe he got to marry this remarkable woman. At last he heard the words. "Jake, you may kiss your bride."

He wrapped his arms around her and lifted her off her feet and kissed her deeply. He prolonged the kiss, until Eli cleared his throat, loudly. The congregation roared with laughter and applause rang out. At last they stood back from each other with shining eyes and wide smiles.

Eli raised his brows at his father-in-law and the pastor nodded his approval for Eli to make the announcement.

Eli's face lit up, he gripped his best friend's shoulder and put his other hand on Lydia's arm. He looked at both faces then out to the audience. "Ladies and Gentlemen, it gives me great pleasure to present to you, Mr. and Mrs. Jake Jenkins."

Jake brushed away a tear and squeezed his bride's hand. He kissed her again and shook his head in disbelief.

He turned to the congregation. "My wife and I would be delighted if you'd join us at the café and help us celebrate. Hannah-Mae has graciously offered to open it especially for us."

Applause rang out and Eli turned to Jake and slapped his back. "Well done, Jake. You made the right choice. I knew you'd see that the right woman for you was there all along."

"Thanks, Friend." The men embraced.

With a final nod to his friend, Eli turned to embrace Lydia. "Congratulations, Mrs. Jenkins. I'm thrilled for you both, he's a good man and you are the right woman for him."

She grinned as he released her. "Thank you, Eli."

Jarrod walked up and punched his brother square in the arm. "You sneak, how'd you keep this a secret?"

Jake was too happy to be angry at him, he rubbed his arm. "Wasn't easy."

Jarrod grinned and thrust his arms around his brother. "I'm pleased for you. She's absolutely the right choice. Well done, Jake."

"Thanks, Little Brother."

Jarrod kissed Lydia's cheek. "Welcome to the family, I'm pleased to have you as a sister."

"Thank you, Jarrod. Thank you Vi." She embraced Vi who lay her hand on her very round abdomen.

Jake looked into the pale blue eyes of his mother. Tears ran down her cheeks. He frowned. "Ma?"

"Son." She smiled and threw her arms around him. "Oh, Son." She wept. "I'm so pleased for you. I'm so pleased for you."

"Thanks, Ma. I'm sorry for keeping it from you."

"I don't mind at all. I'm just so glad for you, after everything you've been through."

"Thanks, Ma. I love you very much."

She raised her brows. "I understand now why you wore your suit."

He grinned. "Had to look good for my bride." He wrapped his arm around Lydia's waist. "Although, I can't compare to her beauty." He kissed her cheek.

"I'll stay with Jarr and Vi for a week," Elsie offered.

He nodded. "I appreciate it, Ma." He kissed her cheek.

Elsie turned to look at Lydia. "Lydia, Darling. You're most welcome. I'm over the moon."

Lydia smiled. "Thank you, Ma. I'm very happy."

They embraced tightly.

Elsie squinted at her son and then turned to grip Lydia's arm. "I'm just sorry we didn't get to throw you the big wedding you deserve. I hope you don't feel deprived of that." She screwed up her mouth.

"Not at all, Ma. I would've married Jake in the general store, a marriage is far more important than the details of a wedding. I just love him so much, I can't believe we're finally married."

Elsie embraced her again. "I love you, Dear. Thank you for making my son so happy."

"Thank you, Ma. He makes me happy too."

*   *   *   *

Jake lifted his wife down from the wagon and placed her feet on the ground. Jarrod would take care of the amphibians later so he flicked the rein over the hitching post and grinned like a lovesick schoolboy. He scooped Lydia up into his arms and carried her up the stairs; pushed open the door and walked inside, turned and pushed the door closed.

Jake kissed Lydia passionately and placed her back on her feet. "I can't believe it. You're finally my wife."

"I'm so happy, Jake."

"You make me happy, my darling. Thank you for making the decision so easy in the end."

"What do you mean?"

"You let me go, you were so gracious. I should've known from that moment it could only ever be you.

I'm so sorry for wavering. Thank you for forgiving me. Thank you for loving me so much more than I deserve."

"Thank you for loving me and rescuing me."

"Well, Mrs. Jenkins. Are you ready for the rest of our lives together?"

"Oh, yes, Jake, of course. I can't wait to spend the rest of my days with you. Thank you for choosing me."

A wry smile crossed his face. "Thank you, Wyatt McCain"

Lydia frowned at him. "Why would you thank Wyatt?"

"Because if it weren't for him you wouldn't have come here, I wouldn't have knocked you off the boardwalk and I wouldn't be so blissfully happy today. So, as awful as he was, I'm grateful that you're here. I'm so in love with you and your incredible eyes." He stroked her cheek. "You're so beautiful, Mrs. Jenkins." He grinned at her.

"Oh, Jake, it's so wonderful to be Mrs. Jenkins. I'm the most blessed woman in the world." She looked around. "I can't wait to make a home for you here."

Jake kissed her deeply again and pulled her into his arms. "Welcome home, my darling."

She lay her head against his chest. "It's a beautiful house."

"No, I don't mean the house. I mean my arms. No matter where we live, where we go, all our days, my arms will always be your home."

"I never want to leave them."

He pulled back from her and cupped her cheek, looked into her mesmerising mismatched eyes and grinned. Slowly lowering his head he brought his lips to hers and closed his eyes. Their hearts sang to each other as they sealed their love with a passionate kiss. His heart sang with joy, there was absolutely no doubt in his mind that he'd made the right choice.

THE END

NEXT BOOK IN THE SERIES: Silas's Brides, by P. Creeden.

Bounty hunter, Silas Jones has never had any interest in marriage until he expressed interest at his family Thanksgiving. Then his mother and his sister each send him a bride at the same time!

Amazon link:
https://www.amazon.com/gp/product/B0CLGVWDY8

Link to readers facebook page:

https://www.facebook.com/groups/576842 341187371

About the Author

Jo Dawson grew up on a dairy farm in Wellsford, a small town in the North Island of New Zealand. She spent fifteen years as a teacher in New Zealand and abroad, before becoming a stay-at-home mum and completing her graduate degree in Theology.

She has lived in Australia and the USA for a time, and these experiences have added to her love of people and history. Blessed with a vivid imagination and the love of classical literature and historical fiction, Jo virtually grew up best friends with Anne Shirley, romping with Jo March and her sisters, sailing a raft down the Mississippi with Huckleberry Finn or living in the 'little house' with Laura Ingalls.

Born and raised in a strong Christian family, Jo's faith is at the centre of who she is, with a lifetime of being involved in churches and Christian camps. These two loves, literature and the Lord, have inevitably converged into writing compelling stories of strong Christian women, courageously facing the hardships of life on the frontier. It is her hope that women of all ages would find encouragement from her heroines' experiences that, while fiction, so often mirror even our modern lives.

Jo currently resides in the small North Island town of Waipu in New Zealand, where she lives with her husband, son, father-in-law and a very lazy cat.

Other books by J. L. Dawson

Journeys of the Heart Series

Awakening of the Heart
Shepherd of the Heart
Decisions of the Heart
A Home for the Heart
Blessings of the Heart
Legacies of the Heart

Douglas Falls Series

Prequel: The Cost of Duty
A Duty to Love
Twixt Duty and Love
A Duty to Family

Multiple Author Series (Standalone books).

Hers to Redeem Book 14: Aaron's Anguish
Hers to Redeem Book 18: Mitchell's Misfortune
Hers to Redeem Book 21: Robbie's Roaming
Hers to Redeem Book 22: Rueben's Risk

Winning His Devotion, Book 8: Ezra's Duty

Second Chance Groom Book 9: Romancing the Attorney

Double Trouble Book 10: Jake's Brides

Standalone Books

To Love Nate – A Companion to Aaron's Anguish.

Where to find these books:

https://www.amazon.com/stores/J-L-Dawson/author
www.jodawsonauthor.com to sign up for my newsletter
jldawsonauthor@yahoo.com to write to the author
Jo Dawson and **J. L. Dawson Author**
-on Instagram and Facebook